MJ QUINN was born in America a[nd]
England, not far from the Atlant[ic]
with a leading intellectual propert[y]
His education has included libera[l]
and legal courses in the UK. In addition to legal and fiction
writing, he has been involved in the theatre.

HOME TURF

MJ Quinn

THE
BLACKSTAFF
PRESS

BELFAST

First published in 2003 by
Blackstaff Press Limited
4c Heron Wharf, Sydenham Business Park
Belfast BT3 9LE
with the assistance of
the Arts Council of Northern Ireland

MJ Quinn has asserted his right under the
Copyright, Designs and Patents Act 1988
to be identified as the author of this work.

Typeset by Techniset Typesetters, Newton-le-Willows, Merseyside

Printed in Ireland by ColourBooks Limited

A CIP catalogue record for this book is available from the British Library

ISBN 0-85640-735-6

www.blackstaffpress.com

To the cousins –
Annie (still with us in spirit),
Anne, Helen and Mary,
and their families, for the unconditional
friendship and support.

Within our souls we harbour intimations of
things we ought to have learned,
people we should have known, and
the lives we might have lived.

We are our own ghosts.

1

'SING ME A SONG, TOM'

'Tommy,' his voice spoke from the phone. Sing me a song, Tom.'

'Dad?' It was the middle of the night – an odd time for my father to call. And an even odder way for him to greet me. 'What's up, Dad?'

But there was no answer. Only peaceful, dead silence.

The days had advanced well into October, well into the depths of autumn. Autumn evoked memories of my youthful years in the academic world – draughty, noisily heated dormitories, stuffy classrooms, and hours spent in library stalls with rich, old, disintegrating books. There was a rawness to living then, when freezing winds and early snows were valued almost as much as the protection of four sheltering walls. But that was years ago. Since I'd become ensconced in the working world, thick sweaters, jeans and boots had given way to suits, overcoats and 'casual business' clothing. The first snowflakes of the season were something

I saw through thirty-fourth-floor office windows rather than in long walks across campus. I missed the intellectual stimulation of academia and the excitement of being constantly out and about.

This October I watched again the changes in skies left grey by the sun's migration, in ambers and browns of leaves. I smelled the changes – the distinct, almost musky aroma of dying leaves on the ground, the occasional log fire, the crisp, biting air – and I heard the crunch of frost underfoot. Somehow, some part of my psyche was recharged and autumn once more brought to mind forests primeval and intimations of immortality.

Halloween was approaching. Not a horrifying time of year, yet a time for dead thoughts and dormant dreams to revive. A time for transitions – transitions I couldn't have anticipated.

The first portent of change was the phone call from Dad, which came some days before Halloween, when I was soundly asleep in my apartment in Hull-on-Hudson. I had been jolted awake by the brash ringing of the phone. I twisted myself out from under bedcovers and plodded clumsily over scattered shoes and clothes to reach the extension in the hallway.

'Hello,' I answered, ridiculously trying to sound alert, like I'd been up and running on all cylinders in the middle of the night.

The other end of the line was clear of static or any background noise. Yet I knew someone was there. The eerie sensation slapped me suddenly wide awake.

'Tommy ... Sing me a song, Tom.' Then there was silence.

There was no mistaking Dad's voice. No one could have imitated the manner of his speaking. No one else really knew the natural, native accent he only used at home.

I cleared my throat. I whispered, then repeated at normal

volume: 'Dad?'

But there was no response. No hang-up click. No dial tone. Nothing but a clean, still-connected phone line.

I spoke again. 'What's up, Dad?'

Silence. Peaceful, absolute silence.

I hung up the receiver – calmer than one might expect. I stood, barefoot and undressed on the wooden floor, feeling the cold boards, the chilly night air, unattuned to distant traffic outside or settling creaks in the building. Something must be wrong. Or at least out of kilter. Yet I didn't feel there was anything I could or should do. Unusual though it was, the call did not induce panic. 'Sing me a song, Tom,' he'd said quietly, not with need or despair.

Later in the morning, squinting under grey daylight and slowly awakening over a cup of black coffee, I was better able to rationalise the mysterious phone call. Could it have been a dream? No. A hallucination brought on by an excess of antihistamines or decongestants? Definitely not; I hadn't taken anything. No, there was nothing to have muddled my mind. Everything about the phone call was clear and real. The problem was undoubtedly a faulty transmission – still not uncommon in overseas calls. And my dad, Michael Rory McDermott, was across the Atlantic Ocean at that time. He'd returned to where he had grown up, in a place called Magilligan in Ireland – technically Northern Ireland, I reminded myself as I looked at the country code for the UK in the phone number Dad had given me. I tried ringing the number. No answer.

In my work, I think clearly and logically. In my personal life, I can be a bit of an idiot. That's why it didn't occur to me until I returned home in the evening that I might track down a number for one of Dad's brothers. By then, however, I'd talked myself into believing that I was mistaken about what I'd heard. If anything were wrong, I convinced myself, I would receive a follow-up call, a proper phone call from Dad or my uncles. Anyway, with my late stay at work and the time change between East Coast America and Ireland, it would be much too late to try calling them or my father. And my reason for contacting them seemed sillier as the hours passed.

Ultimately I decided to wait for the weekend, when I could phone from home at a reasonable hour and with time to chat with old Dad and amuse him with my telephonic hallucination. By the weekend, however, I'd dismissed the whole business as nonsense.

As things turned out, I should have believed my gut feelings instead of rationalising. A few days later I heard that all was not well. When I returned home from picking up the Sunday paper and my usual coffee and bagel, the answering machine greeted me with a message from a Sergeant Norris, of Westchester County, New York's Hull-on-Hudson police force. The recorded voice told me he'd received a call from police in Ireland, concerning a family matter, and suggested that I should call or preferably stop by the Hull police station at my earliest convenience.

I decided I'd follow up on Sergeant Norris's phone call in person, as he had recommended. And best to go at once.

'Thomas McDermott,' I introduced myself to the sergeant.

'Thanks for coming in. I apologise for having to leave a message. I had a patrol officer try you at home, but you were out. Then we got busy with an accident on the interstate.' He led me past a bleak, empty interrogation room into a private office. I declined the offer of a cup of coffee.

'I'm sorry, Mr McDermott,' he sighed. 'It's bad news, I'm afraid.'

'Something about my father then? Michael McDermott?' In answer to the sergeant's questioning look, I explained. 'It would have to be, wouldn't it? He's been in Ireland for a few months.'

'Northern Ireland's where we got the call from,' he clarified.

'County Derry, right. Magilligan. My dad's brothers are there.'

The sergeant looked at his notes. 'The call came from a place called Limavady. Borough of Limavady. Magilligan is in their jurisdiction.' He paused. 'The officer reported that they found a body there, in Magilligan, on the beach. The "strand", he said. The deceased was carrying a driver's licence that identified him as a Michael McDermott. ... There was no question of trying to revive him; he had been dead for some time. The police there located some other McDermotts in the neighbourhood, your cousins, I guess, who verified the identification. Those individuals knew he had a son in America, named Thomas, and after a while one of them remembered the name Hull in New York State. So, their police called here to have us find you.' He paused again. 'My condolences, Mr McDermott.'

I nodded numbly. 'When?' I asked. 'When did this happen?' Although I heard the news that my father was dead, I couldn't take in the meaning. Except on some clinical level. Not emotionally.

'I'm not sure, with the time change,' Sergeant Norris answered. 'My impression is that it was either the same day, or at least within the same twenty-four hours, from when they found the body until they called here. And they think he might have been dead for two or three days.'

'How did he die?' If I let my journalistic training focus on the details, I could get through this interview.

'That I can't tell you. The Limavady crew doesn't know yet. They do say, though, that there's no indication of violence.'

I nodded dumbly.

I was stunned – by the news, of course, but also by the awareness that I'd actually had the news broken to me some time ago. A few days ago, the sergeant had said. Were it not for the suspicion it would undoubtedly arouse, I might have told him the precise day – Thursday, in the late hours of the night, or possibly the early hours of Friday morning, two days ago, when the phone rang in my apartment.

I couldn't refute the possibility that Dad would try to reach me with his own fatal news, if there was any way he could. It was logical, even if paranormal. Not that Dad had told me in the phone call that he was dead, but then he may not have known he was. I understand that's often the case with the recently deceased. He may merely have been aware of being in some altered state of existence and sought consolation – for himself or for me.

Back at the apartment I put aside any esoteric philosophising about the spirit world and called the number I'd been given for the local police in Northern Ireland. The officer in Limavady who'd phoned Hull, an Inspector Tennent, wasn't in. The person I spoke with didn't have any phone numbers for my uncles right at hand but assured me that I could leave a message about my plans for the inspector, who'd see that the information would be relayed to my family over there. I realised that I didn't have any information to leave, except when I'd be flying out, and I didn't even know that yet. Thinking quickly, I concluded that I probably couldn't get myself together in time to leave that same night. Maybe late the next morning. Maybe not. I had no idea which flights, or which airport I'd be flying into.

'I don't know yet,' I said. Then I remembered Dad mentioning when he went back to Ireland the last time – the last time indeed – that he'd be arriving in Belfast in the morning. 'I'll be there Tuesday morning,' I said decisively. 'Arriving in Belfast. I'll pick up a car there.'

'Right.'

The officer gave me directions to the police station in Limavady, where, he assured me, details on how to contact my family would be left for me. He imagined they'd hold off the funeral until I arrived, but he'd be sure to pass along that request as well.

I thanked him and hung up.

I had to go, no question. I had to go to where my dad was. I had to see him. I had to plan the funeral, if his brothers hadn't already done so. And the burial. Would he want me to bring him back to Scranton? I supposed it would be up to me to make those final decisions. And to notify all the appropriate people in America, that would be my responsibility as well.

I started with Mom, who'd been divorced since I was a teenager. I told myself that I really should break the news in person but a trip to Scranton would be well over a hundred miles each way, and I still had to book flights, make arrangements at work, pack. Besides, my parents had been so out of touch since they broke up that I doubted whether Mom even knew that Dad had left Scranton.

'Weaver residence,' she answered the phone.

'Hello, Mom.'

'Tom. How nice. You're not calling about Thanksgiving, are you?'

'No, Mom. I just received some bad news. From overseas.' I hesitated before telling her the only way I could – straightforwardly. 'Dad's dead. He was visiting in Ireland.'

I braced myself for the usual chastisement that 'Dad' meant her new husband, but, for once, she resisted the argument. Mom only said, 'I'm so sorry, Tom', and the way she said it – quietly, after an uncharacteristic pause – actually made me shiver. With an eloquence I never credited her, my mother's tone, bearing the slightest catch in her voice, told me she was really sorry for his death, finally sorry perhaps for the bitterness, sorry for all that had gone wrong with their marriage. I gave her the few bits of information I'd received and I promised to call her from Ireland with additional details.

Then there was my sister Sharon – stepsister, actually, the daughter of Carl, Mom's new husband. From the days when we shared an existence under the roof provided by her father and my mother, Sharon had been the closest friend of my adolescent years (with scarcely a year's separation in our ages), the object of a love–hate relationship, my not-quite-blood-related sister. Once Share (my pet name) was married and had started having children, she began her own matri-archy. While Mom's concept of a core family emphatically excluded ex-spouses, Sharon's perception of her extended family included both me and my real father. After a few years of bickering and compromises over holiday-hosting, Mom further narrowed her definition of family to mean only herself, Carl and the children they'd begot together – basically, her second-rank family (whom Sharon and I maliciously referred to as the second string). And so Sharon had got to know my dad quite well.

When I phoned Sharon, she took in the unexpected announcement with a calm pause, then offered her honest sympathy. I swear I could feel the phone tremble in her hand as she took the news to heart. Her teary voice recalled what my father had come to mean to her and I was gratefully surprised by how much detail she'd retained of their encounters over the years. Her fondness was genuine.

After a while she stopped crying and launched into a barrage of practical considerations that reflected her on-the-job training in motherhood, as applied to my situation. Had I booked my flight? Did I know I should ask for a funeral rate or sympathy rate or grief rate or whatever the airlines called it these days? Could I get the time off from work – of course I could, my father had died, for God's sake! Did I need anyone to watch my apartment, to drive me to the airport? Was there anyone she should notify? Anything she could do?

No, I said to the last questions. I only had Diedrich's Department Store left to notify, the store Dad had once run, once developed into a small chain extending from a home base in downtown Scranton into other parts of northeastern Pennsylvania. Diedrich's was where I'd spent summers working on the sales floor and later clerked in personnel, where Sharon too had worked for odd periods before her marriage and again for a while until the kids starting coming.

'What about the newspapers?' Sharon asked. 'Do you have an obituary you can give them?'

'Best wait till we know about the funeral,' I said. 'I'll phone them when I have something.'

Everything else fell into place. My flights were quickly booked, car reserved, passport in order. I was able to get a photocopy of the police department's record of the call from Ireland, in case I needed it to secure the death-of-a-family-member flight rate.

I never did establish communication with my father's brothers before I left for Ireland. I thought about it. It might have been more efficient if I had phoned ahead to find out what arrangements had been made or needed to be made. But, as much as I favour efficiency, I often yield to instinct. I felt uncomfortable with the thought of introducing myself to my uncles by phone – especially under the circumstances. I sensed that the first meetings with my father's family needed to take place in person, over there, on the family's home turf.

2

GEARING UP

I'd not yet dealt with the tragedy emotionally. I was still reacting clinically – handling the details, preparing for travel. I had neither the time nor the inclination to dwell on these sudden inconvenient tasks, but there I was. I had no choice. But soon I'd be facing the reality of my father's death head-on.

The next morning I awoke at three o'clock – trying to force my internal clock to recalibrate to the time zone of my destination – and began packing. I had time for breakfast at an all-night doughnut shop and was back home to shower and shave. Five minutes to clear the fridge of perishables. Five minutes more to finish packing toiletries and decide which jacket to wear – and another five minutes when I realised I had to find a suit dark enough and a tie sombre enough for a funeral. Then a cab to the train station and an early morning's nap on the Metro-North train until it reached Grand Central station.

As much as I thought I'd been taking my time until then, I was still at my office in mid-Manhattan ridiculously early. I was arts and entertainment editor at *Heights*, a magazine that had evolved from a neighbourhood newsletter into an international periodical. All the departmental editors, like myself, were required to be competent journalists as well as managers, so I was concerned about taking time off.

I caught Ellie – Eleanor Prosser, the office early bird, the editor-in-chief and my immediate boss – in her office before she'd taken off her coat. She looked at me and glowered, anticipating the worst from seeing my face at that early hour.

'What's the trouble, McDermott?'

'My father died. Overseas. I'll need some time away.' It was best to grab her attention with a pithy condensation of the news to start, then fill in the relevant details.

'When?' she asked. Giving her the benefit of a doubt, I took her question to be when did he die, not when did I need time off.

'A few days ago, but he was only found yesterday.' I continued, '"Cause unknown at this time," I was told. Unofficially, the police said he probably died from natural causes.'

'Heart problems?'

'Not that I've ever known.'

By this time, we were both sitting. Ellie was behind her desk, tapping a pen on its surface – a harmless habit that replaced chain-smoking. I was waiting for her to digest the news and its implications relative to *Heights* magazine.

'Do you have a flight to . . . where?'

'Belfast. I'll be staying outside Derry. I'm on a waiting list but I'm going to run over to the airline office to see whether I can finalise the booking this morning. I have a few other errands – an hour, hour and a half's worth.'

'What time are you leaving?'

'Six o'clock should be early enough.'

'Right.' A final bounce of the pen before she laid it flat on the desk. She picked up her empty coffee cup and I followed her to the lunchroom coffee machine. 'Meeting at two in the conference room. No, my office. You, Jack, me. We'll make it a late lunch. Ask my secretary to order in. In the meantime, take care of your errands and work up a game plan with Jack.'

'Right, boss.' I turned to go back to my office.

'Tom?' she called.

I turned.

'I am sorry about your father.'

'Thanks.'

I was halfway down the hall when she called again.

'How long will you be away, McDermott?' she asked.

'Don't know,' I half-shouted back. 'A week? Ten days?' So I said, but I was hoping I'd only need a few days away.

'Humph,' she grumbled behind her cup of black coffee as I vanished around the corner.

The police report paid off at the airline office; I was taken off the waiting list and bumped up to first class to assure my having a seat. I already had a bit of British currency – leftover small change and a few bills that I kept in an open dish on the dresser top. While I was out running errands, I stopped to exchange larger bills. That's when I learned that there are two currencies in Ireland – the British pound and Irish punt. At the risk of being over-prepared, I exchanged for both. What did I know? I was supposed to be going to Northern Ireland, which I knew was part of the UK, but I didn't have a clue whether I'd have to cross the border into the Republic of Ireland.

The rest of the day was filled by a series of meetings and conferences. First, the lunch meeting (Chinese takeaway, what else?) with Prosser and my assistant, Jack Hanan, for a quick review of our department's outstanding projects.

Following on the heels of the luncheon was an editorial meeting neither Ellie nor I had remembered. Some projects I was able to finish in the office, others I packed to take with me.

The activity was nonstop and I didn't expect to have time to really think about my father's death until I was on the plane, dozing from vodka and fatigue – hoping to sleep through an unsavoury meal and a second-rate movie I'd never pay to see, and those annoyingly speeded-up music videos and audio recordings whose sounds cut in and out. Unexpectedly, the first quiet time came long before then, when I was still in the office and had accomplished all the urgent tasks a full hour before I needed to leave for the airport.

As I sat undisturbed at my desk, my attention shifted away from my environment, away from the midtown view from the window. Some song I couldn't identify was running in my mind and brought on a smile. Dad's legacy. Always music – singing, humming, playing the piano, playing records. Could that have been part of what caused their marriage to break up?

Dad had been an excellent provider. He made good in business to give his family all he could in comfort, but he was not concerned with an upper-middle-class image or the trappings of the cocktail set. Was singing through the house part of the comfort he sought to provide, his best means of expressing affection? Was the behaviour too inappropriate to (or an inadequate replacement for) the image Mom sought to present to her targeted circle of acquaintances? I preferred Dad with a song, myself. In younger years, I used to think that all tenors – Irish tenors, specifically – were defined by a flat-voiced, nasal Irish-American tenor who regularly appeared on TV. Not so, my father explained; he introduced me to the recordings of many fine singers, classical and popular. Dad himself had an excellent tenor voice, which I later realised, proudly, I had inherited.

When I was very young, when there were the three of us before the divorce, Mom would tuck me into bed at night and read me a story. And if I hadn't been too much of a brat that night, Dad would re-tuck me in. Occasionally he'd drop a titbit about some childhood exploit of his own or how something I did reminded him of one of his brothers. I was sometimes as serious as Robbie, he might say, or I had Jamie's sense of humour. Only a few remarks about himself and his family in Magilligan, then a gentle 'that's enough for tonight' if I asked too many questions, trying to extend the last few minutes of the day before surrendering to sleep. Nearly always, and especially if Mom was downstairs, he'd softly sing me a song or two.

I wish now I had asked more about his family, his life in Ireland. I wish I'd shown an interest when he was alive. My face and ears burned with guilt. I should have realised what the mysterious phone call was, I should have known something serious was wrong. I should have kept closer in touch. I should have been there with him. Maybe I could have prevented whatever it was that had happened.

I found myself wiping my eyes. Dad was dead. He had always been my home base, no matter where he lived. He was my only constant. In my unmarried, egocentric existence, he was the one person I relied on to take me in – house me if I was between apartments, feed me if I was between jobs. More importantly – most importantly – he was there with silent support if I'd done something incredibly stupid, had made a devastatingly bad investment, had been in an accident, had walked out or been fired from a job. He was there, ready to accept the explanations he never asked for. And if another romance fell apart, he knew and was nearby – sometimes with a song at the old piano in his place, sometimes with a listening ear or a sympathetic shoulder. 'Tommy,' he might say, 'just imagine the worst that can happen from this break-up. The absolute worst. You may never find the one person you could love until death. So what if that's the case? Then you'll work, hard but well. You'll write. You'll take up some hobbies, travel, do things on your own which you might never be able to do as part of a couple. You'll be kind to strangers and animals. Every now and then married friends will invite you to dinner out of friendship and maybe a bit out of sympathy. Would that be so tragic?'

He could make me smile with that. I found his philosophy did help – his imagining the worst possible scenarios, making them still worse until they became at least comic if not downright absurd, then contrasting them with reality.

But, at this time, I couldn't find a contrasting reality less grim than Dad's death.

3

ON THE ROAD HOME

Ireland – both North and South – was virgin territory for me. Although Dad mentioned his brothers there, and his mother, who was still alive when I was a toddler, he never spoke about that divided country as such.

Apparently Dad's being born and raised in Ireland was a mixed blessing for him. He was welcomed into Irish-American organisations, but sometimes he was also expected to show favouritism to businesses (typically suppliers to Diedrich's Department Store) owned by Irish-Americans – as I suppose is true for successful members of most any ethnic group. That was one of several reasons why he would never change the name of Diedrich's to McDermott's. And while his work ethic bespoke intelligence and capability, he still had to fight against stereotypes of being hard-drinking and full of blarney. To be accepted, he couldn't sound too Irish. Thus, he made a point of mimicking a more American-sounding accent, or at least a relatively accent-free pronunciation based on the Queen's English, the British English he'd heard on radio and television while growing up amidst the various Ulster accents.

As for Mom, the attraction was that he was exotic compared with her stale, middle-class existence – a perfect object for romantic interest. She was also of Irish extraction, although her ancestors had come to America several generations earlier and all elements of Irish culture had been watered down to insignificance. He was ambitious. In the long run, however, their ambitions reflected different priorities. He sought happiness in the comforts of home and family, she in the trappings of apparent wealth.

So it was that what little I knew about Ireland was what I had gathered from public Irish-American festivities and from occasional news reports. My perceptions were based on stereotypes. I figured that Dad was merely an exception. I had no desire to learn more about those Irish people whose history was based (according to the bad press I was exposed to as a child) on uncompromising attitudes and violence. Had Dad been aware of my misconceptions, he surely would have taken the time to teach me some truths, but as far as he ever knew I was simply uninterested in our Irish background and homeland.

While I'd come to be open-minded and generous in much of my thinking, it took a long time to overcome childhood-learned prejudices against my own ethnic background. In my adult life I eventually admitted that the Ireland I saw in photographs appeared to be a lovely, incredibly green country worth having a look at and that all Irish people certainly could not fit the stereotypes I'd found detestable. If I kept my ears open, I heard Irish songs that were tender and beautiful and had nothing to do with leprechauns or hard liquor, or violence. If I kept my eyes open, I read and watched reports of Irish Catholics and Protestants falling in love with their own and with each other – admittedly, often against a background of hostilities – and of natives speaking openly against bigotry and terrorism in their country. And in the work at *Heights* I came to recognise a significant number of brilliant Irish-born actors and singers and writers who carried no political agenda into their work. Surely they couldn't all be exceptions. Perhaps the stereotypes were the exceptions?

Still, I hadn't found the time, hadn't made the effort to find the time, to visit Ireland. Until now. To bury my father.

I flew into Belfast International Airport, hired a car and drove towards County Derry. Other than being delayed at the airport until mid-afternoon, waiting for my luggage to arrive on the next flight, I was beginning to feel quite comfortable in my first-time visit to this country. The British currency, driving on the left and the entire road system with signs marked in miles were as familiar as though I were travelling in England.

As I drove northwest along the motorway I was reminded a bit of the countryside hours north of London. The differences were subtle. The infrequent houses I saw en route bore some resemblance to English architecture. Hills rolled away in every direction – not many trees, yet the hills were remarkably green, unless I was deceived by the darkening sky.

When I lowered the car window I breathed deeply the clean, invigorating air. There was an aroma of life, an organic richness that must have emanated from the soil. Already I felt tension loosen from my shoulders.

Some fifteen or twenty miles short of Derry city, I turned north off the A6 and was soon entering the town of Limavady. I parked outside the fortified gate controlling entrance to the police station. The Royal Ulster

Constabulary. Tall walls and barbed wire surrounded the building.

'It's good you came here first,' said Inspector Tennent when we'd introduced ourselves. I thought he was referring to bureaucratic formalities that had to be got through. He assured me, though, that there were no really official tasks ahead – not as far as the police were concerned. I didn't completely understand.

'I'd rather get the next bit over, if you don't mind,' I said, declining an offer of coffee or tea. 'Can I see my father now?'

'Sorry?' he responded.

'Should I be going to the morgue now? Don't I have to identify the body?'

He smiled gently – not, I was glad, with condescension. 'I should have explained. There was no reason to keep your father in the morgue. Bodies are turned over to the families as soon as practical. Your uncle identified your father; the body was turned over to him and his son.'

'And there was no investigation?' I asked. The whole procedure sounded too simple. My father was suddenly dead. There ought to be more to the business than simply saying yes, he died.

'Not in the sense you're probably thinking. One of the local people was out on a morning stroll. He found the body and phoned us. I went out with the team, as did the police doctor. There was no sign of foul play, nothing to investigate – outside of who he was, and whether he was under a physician's care. Which, of course, he was.'

'He was?'

'You did know about your father's illness?'

'No,' I answered. 'He wasn't as active as he was twenty years ago. He was getting a little older, that's all. He was retired. No illness that I was aware of.'

The inspector's matter-of-fact tone was intended to ward off any hysterics. 'He was under regular medical care – here and, according to the labels on his prescription drugs, back in America.'

'His prescription drugs?' I repeated.

'Yes. At the house . . . your father's house, in Magilligan. Robert McDermott, your Uncle Robert, had keys, you see, for emergencies, and he authorised our search. We were looking for the name of your father's doctor specifically because there didn't appear to be anything suspicious about the death.' He let that information settle in before continuing. 'Then we consulted with his physician – a specialist in Belfast. He was a private patient.'

'And?' I wanted to know exactly what the police found, what I didn't know, about my father's illness.

'And? Yes, of course, the cause of death. Cancer, I'm afraid. Lungs. Well past the stage where it could be effectively treated. He instructed his physician he didn't want any extraordinary measures taken to keep him alive. Could be why he didn't tell your family about it.'

'That was it then? He died from the cancer? Shouldn't he have been in a hospital, if it was that far advanced?'

'The cancer was the underlying cause, but it had not advanced far enough to incapacitate him on its own. He should have confined himself to bed, at the very least. That's what our police doctor said. What actually killed him was pneumonia brought on by the cancer. He was highly susceptible to it.' He consulted loose papers in the file before him. 'Bronchial pneumonia. Attributable to bronchogenic carcinoma' he read. 'That's the size of it.' He looked up at me. 'My own notes. Still, that's the gist of the medical report.'

Inspector Tennent was concise, efficient. Quite British in his demeanour and speech, I thought. I wasn't sure why he, rather than a lower official, was here talking to me.

'So,' I said, 'there was nothing questionable about my father's death. The cause was clearly medical. Pathogenic.

Why are you on the case?' It was my understanding that an inspector need not be involved in such mundane, unsuspicious police work.

'There is no case,' he answered. 'And I'm not on it. My only involvement is that I know some of your family.' He smiled as he rose. 'I'm on the road home soon. I'll take you out to the house. Your cousins will meet you there; it's easier than figuring out addresses in the dark if you don't know the area.'

I nodded. I was less than completely focused. The truth of the matter was that I was still avoiding the real world that encompassed my father's death. Still, if I ever thought I could have coped with the news better thousands of miles away in New York, I would have been lying to myself. There's no way I could have properly assimilated Dad's death without visiting where he died and last lived.

I followed the inspector's car out of Limavady, headed north on a narrow two-lane road still categorised as an A highway.

Dusk and an indecisive drizzle obscured much of the view beyond a long estate wall, a small bridge or two, open fields and sparse gatherings of houses close to the road. We slowed upon reaching a sign indicating the village of Bellarena, though the buildings on either side hardly seemed more clustered than anywhere else along the route. I did notice a small railway station and crossing, followed by a couple of shops and mostly houses. A mile or so farther on, Inspector Tennent turned off onto a narrower road between flat, darkened fields, and soon after, he turned into the yard by a small one-storey house. I followed. When we got out of our cars, the silhouette of a man appeared against the open door.

The inspector addressed him. 'Robbie, this is your cousin from America, Thomas McDermott.'

'Thanks, Harley.' Harley? Friends, obviously, as the inspector had said. 'Hello, Thomas,' he said, turning to me.

'I'm Robert McDermott. Your cousin Robbie.' He was about my age, perhaps my senior by a few years. Even in the limited light that escaped from within the house, I could see a family resemblance.

'How d'you do?' I said, shaking his hand. 'Tom.'

'Sorry we're meeting under these circumstances. We didn't know your father was ill. We might have done something, had we known.'

'Apparently he didn't tell anyone. I didn't know myself,' I said. 'I'm sure there's nothing you could have done.'

'Perhaps not. Even Da didn't know,' he said.

'Your father . . .' I began.

'Also Robert. Your da's brother. The eldest of the lot at that.' It was a bit surprising that Robert, the eldest of the five McDermott brothers, was one of the two of his generation still living. The other was James, Jamie, the fifth born. Curious, that only the eldest and youngest were now alive.

'I'm off,' Inspector Tennent called as he returned to his car. 'Regards to Jane.'

'We'll see you this weekend then?' Robbie asked.

'I'll ring you,' the other man answered. 'Mr McDermott,' he nodded to me.

'Inspector,' I responded. 'Thanks for . . . for your assistance.'

He departed.

'Well.' Robbie turned back to me. 'Should we go in?'

I looked back at the car I'd driven. 'Is it all right to leave it here?'

'Anywhere is fine. The garage has your da's car in it. Yours now. I should have let you know not to hire one. I didn't think.'

I wasn't really listening to him, my cousin. I was looking at the house, the garden. The drive here was mildly interesting and the last few miles might have evoked some emotion, were it not too dark to see. Now, though … Now I was here. I'd never had this kind of experience before: I was standing on the land, the very piece of property, where my family had lived for God knows how long – two, three hundred years? More? Where my dad had lived as a boy, as a young man, and in his last days.

I couldn't go inside yet. Not until I'd checked out the garden and got some sort of bearings. I walked around the house, taking in what little I could. Not many trees about. Not much of a garden either. Like the surrounding properties, this patch was remarkably flat, and, even in dim illumination from the house, remarkably green, with grass at the end of October. The grass was springy, the ground wet; the bottom inch of my trousers soaked up water.

Standing in my father's garden in Magilligan reminded me of my rare walks towards the river, back in Hull-on-Hudson – walks not terribly safe, in air not terribly clean. But I was beginning to appreciate a multitude of differences – obvious ones at first. I took a deep breath and tried to sniff out the direction of the sea.

Robbie, who was sticking close by, spoke up. 'Yes, that's the ocean. The Atlantic's on the other side of the sand hills.' I turned towards the generally northern direction he indicated. 'That's one of Europe's top-rated beaches over there. Blue flag.'

Really? I thought. The Atlantic Ocean's as close as that?

He then pointed towards a faint, orange glow to the west. 'Those are the spotlights around Magilligan Prison. There's a training centre for the British Army as well.' He sighed. 'It's a bit of an eyesore. Still, it's quieter than you'd expect.'

Again I only half heard. Already another scent had captured my attention. The smoky aroma was closer, emanating from a chimney in my father's house. A burning fuel, something like wood, something not entirely unfamiliar. The house had several chimneys, rising above a tiled roof. At the front, an enclosed entry. At the back, a one-room extension with large windows that looked quite modern.

'We can go in through the back,' Robbie said, nodding towards the extension. 'If you're ready.' He'd been following patiently during my exploration.

'Yes,' I answered.

We entered through a back hallway and into the kitchen – an old/new room, with an old kitchen table, old cupboards, and modern appliances – compact European appliances, noticeably smaller than American versions.

'Hi.' I was greeted by a pretty blonde woman, whom I took to be Robbie's wife. 'I'm Jane.'

'Tom,' I responded, accepting her handshake.

'I'm very sorry about your father.'

'Thank you. Both of you.'

'I've just put the kettle on,' Jane said, returning to her work. 'The refrigerator's been cleaned, and you're stocked for a couple of days.'

'Thanks' was all I could manage.

'Do you want me to call Fiona?' Robbie asked. 'Sister-in-law,' he explained to me. 'She's feeding the kids.'

'She'll expect us when we're home,' Jane answered. 'The two of you go in,' she said, nodding towards the next room. 'Show Tom the place, would you, dear?'

The tour was short. Robbie wasn't terribly comfortable about showing me around – perhaps because it was my father's house or because of the circumstances or simply because he didn't know what to say other than pointing out the rooms. On the other side of the kitchen was an old-fashioned sitting room, and a modern study in the large extension behind it. Off a short corridor were a small bedroom, a bathroom and a larger bedroom. Except for the garage, that was the entire house.

Jane turned the keys over to me – to the car, to the house. I stared at them, not fully comprehending that they were keys to my Dad's car and house. Now mine. I put them in the pocket of my jeans, just as I would my own keys. A bizarre, tangential thought popped into my mind that perhaps I should buy a bicycle as well, so I could park my bicycle next to Dad's car in the garage attached to the old family house. In some corner of Ireland where I'd never even been before today. Yes, my thoughts were rambling, but I put it down to jet lag.

We talked over tea – sandwiches and biscuits – about what decisions needed making for the funeral and the burial. Jane, the family organiser, had a mental checklist for everything. I promised to call her in the morning to find out whom I had to contact, whose services I might want to use. I nodded mechanically to everything my cousins said. I felt comfortable enough with Robbie and Jane, as though they were family I'd known all along, but I was suffering from sensory overload. They looked concerned about my state of mind, yet they sensed they should leave. Despite their goodwill and assistance, I was relieved when they'd gone.

I would be fine tomorrow, I told myself. I could handle what I had to then. Tomorrow. Tonight I needed to be alone.

4

THE FRAGRANCE OF WHISKY

When the cousins left, I unpacked my luggage in the larger bedroom at the far end of the house. The room was filled with one big bed, a couple of chests and a wardrobe. Once, amazingly, five boys had shared the space. Not so very long ago. If they were hard to visualise, a framed photograph on the wall captured a glimpse of their personalities. All five appeared in their everyday clothes, caught in leisure activity and stilled for the brief opening of the camera's shutter. On the far left was the eldest – Robert or Robbie, the most serious of the lot, but with an easy smile. Eamon by his side – his hand raised in the start of a wave, perhaps, or to shield the sun. Eamon, who had died in childhood. Next my dad, Mickey. Then Jamie, a year younger than my father, holding a blurred ball he must just have caught. Finally Ben, the second born, still a full head shorter than Robbie. I'd seen a smaller copy of the photo many times before, in an album. The framed print on the wall had been enlarged to thrice the size. Here, in this house, in this room, the boys breathed life. The bedroom furniture had been replaced long after the boys had occupied this room. Or so I thought, until I opened the old wardrobe by the fireplace. There, on an inside door, etched by penknife and ink, were the brothers' first names in age rank: Robert, Benjamin, Eamon, Michael, James.

Already the house felt familiar. If I closed my eyes, I could undoubtedly navigate my way through the rooms without bumping into walls or furniture. If I reached for a light switch, it would be where I expected to find it, as would dishes and glasses in the kitchen cabinets, and bath towels in the hot press in the hall. The layout of the house and its accoutrements was simple, based on convenience rather than style.

After a hot shower to purge myself of aeroplane odours, I dressed in my typical leisure garb of shorts and a T-shirt, popped out the contact lenses, put on the glasses, and geared myself for the evening's tasks. As though it were my custom, I grabbed a log of turf, tossed it into the study's fireplace and lit the fire. I must have remembered Dad telling me that burning turf was cheaper than using processed fuels.

Supplied with a dram of whisky and a sandwich left over from tea, I settled at the desk and began to examine its contents. I found a drawer of neatly marked files. The folders contained no extraneous papers – no random grocery receipts, no scraps with scrawled, unidentified phone numbers. Just the relevant material. Documentation about refurbishment of the house – plumbing, flooring, fixtures, new appliances – revealed that all the work, including the addition of the study, had been undertaken since Dad's return. Suspicious, that. He'd told me that he was going back to Derry 'for a while' to visit and look after the old property he'd inherited, but the evidence now in front of me suggested he'd probably planned never to leave again. Other papers confirmed that, except for bank accounts and certain financial holdings, Dad had severed all material ties with America. The files told me more about Dad's past year's activities than he had.

In one of the folders, I found a photo of the house as it must have looked when Dad returned – fallen apart since Grandma McDermott's death, some ten, twelve years earlier. Holes in the roof, windows broken, wooden frames rotting. The walls were dirty and water-damaged from roof leaks and rising damp. No furniture – was it sold? put into storage? Evidently no one had lived here for all that time. More than empty, the rooms bore an air of desertion.

After an hour's perusal, I set the files aside and moved to the rocking chair to assimilate these new details. The last sandwich was eaten, but I hadn't finished my drink. I revelled in the taste of the whisky and the smell of the slowing-burning peat. I'd only acquired a taste for whisky in recent years, and, like my dad, I was a slow drinker. He could nurse two fingers of whisky through an entire evening – never taking a full drink, only touching the liquid to his mouth, as though he were merely tasting it on his lips. And he bought the smokiest brand of Scotch whisky he could find; most Irish whiskey, he once complained, lacked the peatiness he liked. I could still smell the heavy fragrance, not exactly sweet or pungent. I could taste it now in my drink, and in the air, in the aroma. The flavour of peat.

My God, I never realised! The smoky taste in my father's whisky was peat. Of course. Every sip must have been a taste of home – the peat burning in the fireplace, the peat in the soggy, dark ground, the peat gently infiltrating wells, leaving a fine trace in the drinking water, the bathing water.

I could feel him with me now.

'It would appear, Dad,' I said aloud, taking another sip, 'there's much you never told me.'

I only spilled a drop when I heard my dead father's voice

answer me from behind.

'How could I have explained it all?' he said.

I turned. There sat my father, in the stuffed chair by the fire, as young and healthy as I'd ever known him (more so, perhaps), yet undoubtedly a ghost. Still, I'm not easily at a nonplus. A false image, surely that's what he was. My mind's conjuration.

'So,' I continued, calmly accepting for the present the improbable figment. 'Did you plan this all along?' I waved my arm, encompassing the house's reconstruction.

'Could you spare some of my whisky?' he asked, indicating my glass. I handed it to him. His hold on the glass was real enough; it didn't fall to the floor when I let go. 'I didn't know whether I'd ever come back,' he said. 'Then, when I knew ... well, as they say, knew that my days were numbered – there was nothing to keep me from coming home. From revitalising some of what I'd loved about this place. As much as it could be done, in these times. Not much of a house, still it's all I ever wanted for a home ... I've brought it up to date – you've figured that – to see it into the next century. The firm I hired did a rather good job, don't you think?'

I nodded.

He sipped the drink. 'Excellent.' He nodded towards the living room (or lounge, as he'd say) through the doorway. 'That used to be the kitchen,' he said, 'before the first remodelling when I was very little. I can remember, just barely. What's now the kitchen was one of the bedrooms. It was a very typical arrangement – the kitchen in the middle, a bedroom on one side, a parlour on the other side. Over time the other bedroom, my brothers' and mine, was added on the far side. Plumbing and a bathroom were brought inside. A long time ago now.'

In my mind I pictured the earlier house he described, as though the imprints of the earlier rooms bled through into the present. The ghost of the house as depicted by the ghost of my father.

'It's yours now, you know,' he continued. 'The house, everything here. In trust, mostly, so Robbie can administer everything on your behalf for the time being. But it's yours for the claiming any time you like. The papers are all there' – he gestured to the stack of files on the desk. 'You'll like the car. Good on petrol, which costs more than double what you'd pay back in the States. I might have got diesel, but you're not accustomed to it.'

I laughed. 'It's been a while since I've heard you say so much in a single stretch.' I also noticed that he'd lapsed – permanently, I suppose, or should I say eternally? – into the gentle Northern Irish accent he'd only felt comfortable using at home. I'd heard the accent in Robbie's and Jane's voices as well, and in the voices of other people I'd spoken to since I arrived. Not the heavy so-called brogue of the caricatured Irishman. There was a gentle rhythm in the region's speech, the hint of a song. A melody. A bit Scottish, no question of that. I liked hearing that quality in his voice.

'It's been a while since I've been really at ease. Light-spirited, you might say.'

'What's it like?' I asked before I could stop myself. I had a vague apprehension that it might be a breach of etiquette to ask the dead about their state of being. Or non-being.

He looked aside as he searched for the words. 'Like dreaming,' he said finally. 'You can drift between different levels of consciousness. For example, at this moment I'm entirely focused on being with you in this room. I'm immersed in your reality. I can come and go most any time I like, although it's easier some times than others. But I can also let go completely and . . . diffuse.'

'Vanish, you mean? Disappear?'

'Leave,' he answered. 'Outside this material world, it's possible to go to a place where you can bring into existence anything you can imagine.'

'But it's not real.'

'Not in the sense of earthly reality, no. But it's not false, either.'

I shook my head. 'I don't understand.'

'Neither do I, exactly,' he said, scratching his head and grinning. He shrugged. 'I suppose it's impossible to grasp unless you're there, in that place, that state.'

'And you're not simply a creation of my mind?'

'Who's to say?' He shrugged. 'I feel like myself. Is that something you're capable of projecting?'

He had me there. If I were able to project an external image of what I perceived was my father from his own point of view, how would I know whether this entity was my projection or his ghost? Or could his own projection of himself be drawing the energy for its existence from my empathy? I couldn't answer.

We moved on then to topics more mundane. The household furniture was no great mystery after all. Much of the furniture of Dad's childhood home had ended up in Robert's family's barn or had travelled across Lough Foyle to my Uncle Jamie's house in County Donegal.

'You'll like Jamie,' Dad said cheerfully. 'I imagine he'll bring the whole clan over for the funeral. The Finneys, as well. You've not had the funeral yet, have you? I know nobody has old-fashioned wakes any more.'

'Nothing yet, no. As a matter of fact, I should ask you . . .' I stopped. 'You don't mind talking about all this?'

'Not in the least. Go on. Ask.'

'Do you want to be buried here? Or go back to the States? I didn't know what to do with your . . . with the body. With your remains. Is that in the files somewhere?'

I first mistook the look on his face for consternation. But it was sheepishness. 'I meant to get around to that,' he apologised. 'I don't know. I know you're partial to cremation, but what to do with the ashes? Or a burial up on the mountainside is a possibility. There are some fine views of the valley from the Church of Ireland and the Catholic cemeteries. Not that it matters; we can visit any time, I don't need to be buried up there. But I shouldn't bother sending me back across the ocean if I were you. Wouldn't be any point, would there?' He brightened. 'You've always been a clever boy, Tommy. You can decide. As long as you have something for the family. They'd be terribly put out if they couldn't have a get-together.'

I smiled wryly. 'Thanks heaps, old man.'

He laughed but rose, evidently preparing to leave.

'This talk isn't ... distressing, is it?' I asked seriously, distressed myself that he was leaving me again.

He shook his head. 'The late hour. I'm feeling tired.' He set the whisky glass on the side table. 'Funny. Being with the living is somewhat draining. Don't know why.'

'Right,' I said, rising from rocking chair. 'Blame me. It's all right.'

'You can take it, Tom,' he said, putting his hands on me. 'You've got the broad McDermott shoulders.' His touch, as soon as I felt it, began to lighten as he began to fade. 'Goodnight, son.'

''Night, Dad.'

He was gone, and I was left, drained as well. Did I believe I'd been visited by my father's ghost? Oh, yes. And I realised that since the news of my father's death I'd been waiting for some additional event. The appearance of Dad's ghost was the proverbial second shoe dropping.

I took the empty glass – the only evidence of his visit, if ghosts leave fingerprints – and the sandwich plate to the kitchen, then stumbled the few steps to my bedroom and a long, welcome sleep.

5

ACCLIMATISATION

Thankfully, I slept deeply and restfully. Another man might have tossed and turned through the night, questioning the evening's apparition. But I didn't question what I'd seen. In a battle between logic and experience, I accepted without challenge that my father was a ghost. I'd seen him, talked with him, even felt his touch. I found comfort in the truth.

I awoke early from the solid, revitalising slumber. After a quick shower, I drove out to Magilligan Point, passing the prison and army barracks whose lights Robbie had pointed out to me. Past the Point Bar I parked by the Martello tower, off the deserted road that stopped at the prison fence. I paid no attention to the old tower. My quest was the ocean – on the far side of ridges of dewy-grassed sand dunes.

There lay the beach –empty of people, devoid of litter. Broad stretches of clean wet sand. The waters of the Atlantic Ocean rolled in regular, cold blue, white-tipped waves. The horizon blended the sea with the pale blue, misty dawn sky. The scene was peaceful and timeless. It could have been an ancient, primitive shoreline billions of years before the arrival of the human species.

I walked out to the edge of the water, avoiding the tidal pools slowly disappearing into the sand. Staying safely outside the British Army's red-flagged rifle range, I meandered along the beach, stopping to examine the calcareous armours of whelks and small crabs, which had been pecked open by gulls. I picked up a few specimens – butterfly shells, dog cockles and dog whelks, scallops, limpets, mussels, a couple of razor shells – whatever seemed attractive to me. Many were the same shells I'd once collected as a boy along the Atlantic's American shores, especially the ubiquitous clam (or cyprina or quahog) shells.

I breathed deeply, feeling the bronchi in my chest crackling open as they loosened and absorbed pure, rich ocean air. Those lovely negative ions. I only turned home when I was fully awakened by the wet breeze. And when my jacket pockets were filled with my sandy acquisitions. By that time I was ready to face the day's tasks.

First, over to the cousins' house before Robbie had to leave for work. Breakfast with Jane, Robbie, Robert senior, the kids. A hearty meal – more than my customary black coffee and bagel. Besides toast and lightly scrambled eggs, the breakfast featured fried meats (which I could scarcely stomach looking at, let alone eating) and something called boxty – an interesting grated potato pancake. Top it with a dab of sour cream or apple sauce, I thought, and you've got something there. Like the Jewish *latke*.

The first task after breakfast was returning the car I'd hired in Belfast. I dropped it off at the City of Derry Airport, following Jane there so she could (as she insisted) drive me back to Magilligan.

Back at the house, I looked at the names and numbers Jane

had given me. We were sharing chores. While she would be ringing the *Constitution*, a local newspaper, to post the death notice and would phone all the cousins, I still had to make the funeral arrangements. Robbie had warned me, and my first phone call confirmed, that I'd have to look to Belfast (or Dublin) for a cremation and the timing would be tight. But I managed to arrange it. There would be no viewing, except for my own private visitation.

I drove Dad's car to the funeral home in Limavady.

I didn't care that the body hadn't been 'properly prepared'; in fact, I wanted to see him without mortuary make-up, not tarted up for – well, for a funeral. The corpse I saw lying on a cold metal trolley looked older than my last sight of Dad. And thinner. Colourless. And empty – flattened, deflated. I found it hard to conceptualise the cadaver as my father. No spirit existed in the body, yet that body was all the physical substance that was left of the man I'd known, for my entire life, as a living being. I touched the face. I felt only cold, lifeless organic matter. The ghost who'd visited me possessed more of my father's life and breath than this discarded shell. I could hardly grieve over an empty body when his spirit was with me at home.

My father's body would soon be en route to the crematorium and I'd be there myself later in the afternoon for the paperwork and payment.

In the meantime, I had to arrange some sort of funeral service locally. I suppose I was more stunned by the visit from Dad's ghost than I realised, because I didn't push hard enough for his preferences. He mentioned the views from different churches but that was all. I knew he had been raised Catholic, but his rare visits to church in America were to an Episcopal church. The Episcopal religion was essentially the same as Anglican, I was sure, but there didn't seem to be a clear equivalent in Magilligan. Unless that's what the Church of Ireland was all about. Anyway, it was probably the architecture that was more important to Dad than the religious doctrine. I drove around to look at the Presbyterian Church on the Seacoast Road and the Church of Ireland and Roman Catholic buildings off Duncrun Road, up the hillside. My preference was the RC chapel – for its views over the countryside and the ruins of an earlier church structure. Jane and Robbie agreed with my choice – although on the basis of religious grounds and what the family would expect.

When I finally sat down hours later, in my own house, to the still-warm dinner of tandoori takeaway and a fresh salad, I felt that I'd accomplished quite a bit, due largely to Jane's orchestrations. I'd made the most urgent decisions, I'd arranged the funeral, and I'd managed some household shopping.

'You know,' I said, skewering another forkful of chicken, 'this is not at all bad. You can't find Indian food in Hull. The pickings are not that great in Scranton either, but you know that yourself. Have you tried this, Dad?'

No answer. I wasn't really expecting one. Last night was ... Well, jet-lagged or not, I had been tired. And I'd been drinking. No more than an ounce or two of whisky, granted, but ... Last night was a fluke. Not that I denied my dad's presence, haunting the old family homestead. At the moment though, while the sun remained above the horizon, he was not here. And I had no reason to expect another visit now that I'd settled the funeral events that should give his life closure.

It was time to dig into work – work for the magazine, that is. Yes, I was on leave for a couple of weeks, but I'd promised to finish some projects and to touch base while I was away. In truth, it was a relief, a distraction from my troubles, in which familial obligations were falling neatly into place, while my personal life had become disorienting.

I made my call to *Heights* magazine. While I was waiting for the receptionist to locate Ellie Prosser, I turned on the computer and grinned. Dad had had this computer installed with exactly the same configuration and software as I'd set up for him in Scranton. I wanted to believe he'd anticipated my using it but it was more likely he'd decided to duplicate a set-up that had become comfortable.

'Eleanor Prosser,' a voice finally said.

'Pross!' I said, turning from the screen. 'Tom McDermott. How are things over there?'

'Tom! Are you in Ireland now? What's the number? Where can I fax you? You can squeeze in some work, can't you?'

I gave her the phone number. 'I'll have to find some place to receive faxes. Let me look into it. What's so urgent anyway? Everything's all right with Jack?' My assistant had only been on his own a couple of days.

'Jack's fine. A little overwhelmed maybe, but otherwise fine.'

She explained the problem, which was Simon Morrison, a freelance writer in the political arena – not my field at all – whom I'd inherited by default. Although an excellent resource, Simon was remarkably sensitive about letting anyone but me edit his work. And there was a consensus that his idiom-packed contributions required heavy editing to fit our magazine's style. As one cynical fellow editor once commented, 'Si writes like a sports columnist.'

'So you'll fax me whatever Si sent in. I have his number if I need to clarify anything. When do you need the article finished?'

'Yesterday.'

'Give me a week.'

'You've got it.'

In truth, I was hoping to be finished with both Simon Morrison's article and my dad's funeral by the weekend, and to be back in the office Monday morning.

'I'll let Jack know where to fax as soon as –'

'I want you to do something else,' Ellie interrupted. 'When are you free to travel?'

'Well, the funeral's Friday . . .'

'Jesus, you must think . . . That's why you're there in the first place.' In the momentary pause I could visualise her reaching for a pen to tap on the desk. 'I'm sorry. I mean, I'm really sorry. I should have . . . Is there anything I can . . . Flowers or something? What do they do over there – buy prayers or candles? A mass card, is that right?'

Typical assumption – that all Irish are Catholics. (Ellie missed the other assumption that most everyone in Northern Ireland must be Protestant.) My father's family were a mixture of Protestants, Catholics and what-have-you. Dad himself had only been loosely Catholic and not much of a practitioner.

I laughed. 'I think a donation of some kind might be best. I'll send you the name of a local charity or a school. I think Dad would prefer something like that.'

'Donation. Got it. Now, about the travel. Can you get over to London after the weekend?' I could, I told her. She gave me a sketchy background of a rising young actress who'd just taken over the leading role in a long-running West End musical and was on the brink of public recognition – the moment *Heights* sought to capitalise on.

'Now,' I said when Ellie'd finished her outline and I agreed to fit in the interview, 'about faxing. Maybe I can find a hotel somewhere or a business nearby that will take in a few pages for me. I'll check in the morning.'

'A few pages!' she shouted into my ear. 'This is not good, McDermott. Listen, here's what you'll do. In the morning you'll go find a city – there must be a real city somewhere near you? – and buy a fax machine. Then you'll take it back to your little cottage –'

'Bungalow,' I corrected her, just to be harmlessly contrary.

'– and hook it up to that number you gave me, if you can't get a second line installed right away. I'll call you at eight o'clock in the morning. My time.'

'Make it nine.'

'Eight.'

'All right. Eight thirty.' I sighed. 'And about that donation the magazine's making?'

'Yes?'

'Think very, very big.'

'I know, I know. I'm intruding on your time of grief. I am sorry, truly. It is absolutely unconscionable.' Her voice softened. 'I promise to make it up to you.'

With that, we signed off, before I could ask to be transferred to Jack.

So I wouldn't be back in New York as soon as I'd hoped. Tuesday then. Wednesday at the latest.

I phoned Mom's house after procrastinating as long as I could. Fortunately, she wasn't home, so I could breathe freely and leave a short message on her machine with details about the funeral, ending by mentioning (in hopes that she wouldn't phone back) that I was off to bed.

Sharon was washing up dishes from dinner when I rang her.

'Who have you met?'

'Official people – police, mortician, church. Dad's eldest brother, Robert; he's got to be in his late seventies by now. His son, Robbie. Robbie's family. They all seem nice enough so far – kind of familiar, actually. I can see some family traits. And apparently there are dozens more McDermotts here and in the next county. McDermotts and Finneys.'

'So, what's it like there?' she asked. 'This is your first time in Ireland, isn't it?'

'Yes, it is. It's very much like England – the north of England especially. Very wet.'

'What does the area look like? Is it built up very much?'

'Not at all. To tell the truth,' I admitted, 'I've hardly had a look around. It's all been back and forth between here and Limavady.'

'Limavady? Where's that?'

'Limavady's what I guess you would call the borough seat. Not much of a town by any standards, but it has its own charm ... There's a great old pub that hasn't changed in centuries. And locally we have Binevenagh for interest. That's the mountain overlooking Magilligan. It's deceptively small but it does loom and can look especially ominous when the fog's hanging over it. It has a distinct profile that distinguishes the Magilligan area.'

I realised that, for the limited exposure I'd had to Magilligan so far, it was having an effect. My speech had slowed to a more leisurely pace. Even my muscles were relaxed.

'The beach is wonderful,' I went on, 'despite the disturbing intrusion of a prison and a British Army base. Lots of clean, fine-grained sand. Lots of ocean. We're on the northern Atlantic coast, you know. It's a lovely, quiet beach. At least at this time of year.'

I told Share about the house in Magilligan, now my house, the old photos and furniture, its modern comforts, computer and all, as well as the assignments coming in from *Heights* and the work I had lined up.

'Sounds like you're right at home,' she commented.

I had to agree.

6

JUST AN OLD SONG

In the morning, I expected to be eastbound to Coleraine in search of a fax machine. Coleraine lies farther east along the northern Atlantic coast – a bit inland, actually, straddling the River Bann – and has a certain Northern Irish urbanity. But no, Jane apparently didn't trust my navigational skills, because she sent me back into Limavady with a list, while she made the trip herself to Coleraine for groceries for the upcoming family gathering.

I found my way around fine in our local, increasingly familiar town, although navigating the one-way streets enclosing the two adjacent, dissimilarly sized blocks comprising Limavady's business centre made me feel like I was circling a six-sided square. No matter. I found a suitable fax machine almost immediately, at a shop in the pedestrianised area. With no trouble at all I obtained everything on Jane's list, which were merely dry goods and fresh fruits and vegetables. I even improvised, adding cut flowers on impulse.

Because I'd done well with the straightforward assignments (and had only returned to the wrong car park once), I rewarded myself with a pint at Owens' public house. I entered the bar in the middle of a conversation, catching one regular's complaint about a business transaction – could have been buying a used car or a generator, I wasn't certain – in which he griped that the seller 'maun' have thought he'd 'come up the Bann in a bubble'.

As an obvious stranger in the pub, I was prepared to be asked where I was from. When I said New York, I was told I didn't sound American. I heard that a lot. The natives seemed to accept my presence, to the point of informing me that the pub regularly received visitors from far abroad – even from Australia and once a busload of Americans from Pittsburgh.

When I explained my connection to their area, the men tried to think of McDermotts they knew, mentioning individuals I hadn't yet met and arguing among themselves whether some particular McDermott family were the ones come from over the hill (towards Coleraine?) in the seventies or were those living up on Duncrun Road. I had to confess that, at that point, I only knew the family of Robert McDermott senior and junior.

'Aye, a good man, Robert.'

They assured me there were McDermotts aplenty in and around the borough, and I was bound to meet a good number of them. Despite their offers, I stopped at one pint, as I was driving.

At home, I filled the refrigerator, reported to Jane, installed the fax machine and worked on my dad's obituary for the newspaper back in Scranton while I was waiting for Ellie's phone call – which came predictably early, at eight twenty New York time – followed by what seemed like a half-ream of fax transmissions, most of which were totally unnecessary. I phoned Jack.

'Did you see what she faxed me, Jack?' I complained. Ellie Prosser was a good boss, but thoroughly excessive when it came to doling out work. Out of control, actually. 'Is there anything here you haven't already taken care of?'

'I'm expecting a few return phone calls,' he said. 'Otherwise, it's under control.'

'So the only thing I really need to worry about, outside of the London interview this weekend, is the Si Morrison editing?'

'And it's all yours, Tom. I wouldn't dream of depriving you.'

'Thanks,' I answered wryly. 'Look, I'll work on it as much as I can this evening. I'll phone or leave you a message in the morning. The funeral's tomorrow, so Si's article should be a good distraction tonight.'

'Tomorrow? Gee, that's Friday already, isn't it?' He sighed. 'Look, how about if I do the first revisions? Give you some more time with your family.'

I shook my head. 'I'll be all right. That's all tomorrow. We're having the ... I don't know what to call it. It's sort of a post-funeral ... something or other. A wake, I suppose, although I've been told that wakes are not really the fashion any more. It'll be at my cousin's, Robbie McDermott. Remind me to give you the number.'

'I'm not going to call you there,' Jack said emphatically.

'I know you're not,' I said. 'As long as you know where to reach me, you won't need to. It's ... what? Not karma, not Murphy's Law.'

'Sounds like a perversion of the Law of Diminishing Returns. The more accessible you make yourself, the less you're needed.'

Not bad, I thought. 'However, you may not, under any circumstances, give Robbie's number to Prosser. I'll talk to her here, if she needs to reach me. But anything she wants to fax me is to go through you for screening. Tell Lorna that too.' Lorna was our secretary.

He groaned. 'Ellie won't like it.'

'No. But she'll give in – throw up her hands, storm out of the room. After a couple of hours she'll ask for your judgement on what I need to see.'

'In the meantime?'

'I'll call her, tell her the procedure is not negotiable. Toss in something about streamlining our efforts to maximise our output. Nothing's quite as good as preposterous bureaucratic posturing. When she starts laughing I'll know she's accepted the arrangement.'

It was only when I rang off from the *Heights* office that I realised how much time I really had to work on my own projects. Jane wouldn't let me help with the preparations for tomorrow; she and her sister were organising everything themselves. Well before the work day was over in East Coast America, I had fleshed out Dad's obituary and was faxing the final version to the *Scranton Sentinel*.

By tea time, I had most of the Si Morrison article rewritten. Retyping the bugger from scratch, with my revisions, helped fill the time. I finished the article before the evening was out and e-mailed the text to Jack clean and grammatically pure – yet entirely true to the original author's style, such as that was.

I was amazed. Without the interruptions of phone calls and people dropping by my office, I could work quite efficiently. I could successfully compartmentalise projects into series of tasks, then work on each discrete portion until completion. As I finished each task, I could move onto another or, when all the immediate jobs were finished, enjoy some free time. Working at home must be like this, I observed, finding myself in an unexpected free period – something I never experienced in the office. What was I supposed to do with myself?

With the computer and fax machine not running, the house was silent. For fresh air, I opened a window facing the unseen ocean. Over the pervasive scent of turf fires, I smelled a light rain coming down, carried inland by a sea-salted breeze. I felt . . . I felt at peace. My attention drifted to the upright piano by the windows. It was new, beautifully finished in oak – definitely not reclaimed from the old home. No signs of wear. Was it ever used? I wondered until I touched the keys myself. It was broken in and well tuned. The choice of wood, the structure of the box, even the placement of the instrument contributed a pleasing wetness to its sound.

I rooted through the neatly tied stacks of sheet music stored under the hinged piano seat – some nearly crumbling with age, others stiffly new. One particular old piece I recognised with fondness. It was deeply creased where the pages had once been folded into quarters. Many years ago these sheets had travelled from this house, traversing the Atlantic and entering Pennsylvania stuffed in the pocket of a jacket worn by young Michael McDermott. The song was 'You'll Never Know' – written by Mack Gordon and Harry Warren, the publication said, and copyrighted in 1943. The sultry-voiced Alice Faye had sung the Oscar-winning song in *Hello, Frisco, Hello*. And I remembered my dad singing it. I used to think it an odd choice for his favourite, until I worked out that he was probably in early adolescence when the movie was released.

I began to play and sing, as best I could, imitating his attention to the words. Holds up well, I thought. When I stopped, I heard only the sound of uninterrupted rain.

'What did it mean to you?' I asked. 'This song.' I wasn't guessing whether my father was there. He hadn't moved on yet. I could feel his presence behind me.

'I don't know,' he answered. 'It was just a song.'

I persisted. 'But you brought it with you. Did it have

something to do with your emigration? Was the song connected with someone you were leaving back here?'

He took the same soft chair as the last time, near the fire. 'It's just a song,' he repeated. 'Already old when I knew it. I may have found the flow of it, the wording, clever. American songs were like that. To tell the truth, I grew to like it better as I got older – when I got past the clever phrasings and into the sadness.' He smiled. 'A nice little ballad, isn't it?'

'You're sad tonight.'

'Melancholic, I suppose. I am being buried tomorrow, aren't I? Doesn't that entitle me to some sort of ... reflection? Maybe a bit of depression?'

'Yes. By all means. But ... ah ... well, you're not being buried, I'm afraid. I didn't think ... You see, I arranged a cremation.'

He waved away my concern. 'Burial, cremation, it doesn't matter. Immaterial to me.' He paused. 'You know what tonight is?'

'Thursday?'

'Samhain.'

'Excuse me?'

'The feast of Samhain. Well, actually the eve of Samhain for a few hours more. Oíche Shamhna. Halloween.'

'Samhain?'

'The Celtic New Year. The beginning of winter. The night when it's unsafe to venture out of doors alone, when the supernatural, the dead, can most easily communicate or interfere with the living. When you go to bed – early to be sure – you should leave a fire in the hearth for your dead ancestors who come calling while you're asleep.'

I took his legends in stride. 'You began communicating a couple of days early yourself, didn't you?'

'A father's privilege, perhaps. Or we're close enough, we're not confined to the minimal allowances. Not that there are such limitations.'

'You never said much before about the old religions. Samhain, is it? And other Celtic traditions.'

He shrugged. 'Somehow, Scranton never seemed the appropriate setting for tales of the old gods and ancient traditions. Would you have believed any of it?'

'Don't know. It's part of my job to master new fields of knowledge most any day. I've got to be open to all ways of thinking in the arts, all philosophies. There's much I believe in.'

'God?' he interrupted.

'Not as such. Too anthropomorphic on the one hand, too omniscient on the other. Gods in the plural, yes, because they're merely supernatural beings whose control of the workings of the universe falls far short of infinite. And they're imperfect, which is more to my liking. The concept of a singular, all-powerful humanoid is too easy an excuse for abandoning personal responsibility. I prefer to think we're all subject to the simple workings of nature . . . And, of course, the extrasensory and supernatural.'

He studied me a moment before he responded. 'They don't let you touch religious topics at your job, do they?'

'No,' I laughed. 'Perhaps, after all, you did fill my innocent head with bedtime stories of paganism.'

'Aye. Perhaps I did,' he said softly. 'You'll find a pervasiveness of the ancient beliefs here. If you took news reports at face value, you might reason that Ireland is satiated with Christianity and the "troubles" are due to theological conflicts between Catholics and Protestants, rather than cultural prejudices, ethnic oppression, imperialism, and . . . I'm digressing. My point is that people don't discuss the old religions as such, they don't talk about the spirits of nature, the fairies in the hillsides and so on, but they're infused into the history and culture nevertheless – the fairies, the giants, the gods and goddesses, the warrior chieftains, the saints and the rebels of legend. Fact and fiction, it's all part of our heritage.'

What he said rang true. Even in America we have our own legends and superstitions – some new, most adopted from the nebulous Old Country – that usually have little to do with established religions. We have multitudes of traditions about birth and marriage and death. We avoid the number thirteen, breaking mirrors and letting black cats cross our paths. We knock on wood, we toss salt over our shoulders, we say 'God forbid' when talking about hypothetical misfortune. We believe that houses built on Native American burial grounds are inevitably cursed. We share campfire stories about ghostly hitchhikers, besieged adolescents driving on isolated roads, psychopathic prison escapees. We believe in Bigfoot, the Jersey Devil, Paul Bunyon, extraterrestrial visitors, the immortal Elvis Presley and Jim Morrison. We make legends of our heroes – be they presidents or movie stars. We believe in good vibrations and bad, and the music of the spheres. We seek enlightenment in Tarot cards and crystal balls and psychic telephone services. We regress to past lives and future lives and alternate existences.

'I believe I understand,' I said. 'The myths, the old lore, never really disappeared from the Irish culture.'

He nodded. Then, in a sudden change of tone, he asked: 'What will you do with the ashes?'

'Your ashes? I thought I'd sprinkle them in the ocean, near the beach. Unless you'd rather I keep everything in the urn?'

'No, no,' he said quickly. 'I like the idea of being strewn along the strand. Do you need to get permission?'

I shrugged. 'Not if I don't tell anyone. I was planning a surreptitious act.'

He smiled again. 'I like that.'

I played the opening bars of the song again. 'Was it hard – leaving home?'

Sombreness returned to his face. He closed his eyes a moment. 'I don't know that I would have gone away, but for the assurance of a job in America. The economy here ... Well, I was twenty-one and there wasn't much here for young people. Even the soldiers who'd returned from the war a few years earlier found the prospects sobering. Some of my mates had already gone ahead – to New York mostly.'

When he stopped, I got up and poured two drinks. When I handed him the glass, his fingers closed for a moment over mine. We were both stricken by the touch. It had probably been years since we'd actually had physical contact, I suppose. I was surprised that I could, now, feel the flesh of his hand as though warm blood were flowing beneath the skin, muscles and tendons flexing, nerves pulsing. Then he took the glass from my hand and the connection was broken. He cleared his throat to break the awkward moment.

'The night before I left,' he went on, 'I was here with the family. There were only me, mum and da, and Jamie. Robbie was already married; I'd stopped by his house earlier. I'd been out with my friends after dinner – in a sort of American wake, like they used to have when sons and daughters emigrated to America – and now they were all home and probably in bed. Jamie was asleep. The old man had gone off to bed, but I couldn't hear any snoring from his room. Mum was sitting in there, in the other room' – he nodded towards the sitting room – 'with a book in her hand. She didn't turn a page all night. While she was not reading and Da was not sleeping, I was barely sipping at a cold cup of tea. There was nothing else to say. We'd gone through all the "did you remembers" and "don't forgets" hours ago. So I sat there. Tasting the tea. Smelling the air, the old house, the furniture. Listening to the same old clock ticking and smelling the faintly rancid oil enmeshed in its gears. Hearing the slightest breeze and, I was sure, the faint sound of steady waves beyond the Doaghs. Everything in the room – the rough walls, the furniture, the lights, windows, doors – burned into my brain.

'Finally I went to bed, but it didn't matter whether I closed my eyes. I couldn't shut out all the images of home. In my mind I walked down the strand, I looked across the lough, I drove into the city, my friends and I carousing as though every moment we spent together were the best ever. While lying in my bed, I climbed Binevenagh and gazed over the flat stretch of Magilligan which I didn't expect ever to see again.

'When morning finally came . . . I left, with a sick feeling, as though I'd drunk too much strong coffee on an empty stomach, as I had.'

I believe I knew something of what he felt. We both felt a deep emptiness inside – my dad from the home he'd left behind and missed, me from a more subtle feeling of home I'd never experienced as he had. The home in my soul was cosy, yet it was limited to the childhood feelings of security – a warm bed, a favourite teddy bear, soothing parental voices. It was a comforting sensation, but lacked . . . history? geography? Was that it? My awareness of home was nearly foetal, with limited visual aspects and no fixed setting. I was just beginning to understand vicariously Dad's perception of home, in this house, in this land. And I envied him it.

7

THE FUNERAL

The morning greeted me with cool air and continuing unintrusive rain. Chimney smoke rising from unoccupied hearths was scant in the early hour, thin and stale from the night before. I drove out to the edge of Lough Foyle, seeing no one, save a fly-fisherman who nodded hello between casts. The clouds had thinned just enough for the sun to build a partial rainbow across the water. The arc grew until the colours became distinct, then faded. Was the rainbow supposed to be an omen? Or was it a marker for the land across the lough, in County Donegal, where the Jamie McDermotts lived? If any of them were up and about now, I might wave a greeting. But I'd see them soon enough.

The dismal weather was appropriate. Although I was neither depressed nor overcome by grief – how could I be when my dead father visited regularly? – sunny skies would have been quite disagreeable on that day.

By late morning I had breakfasted, washed, changed into respectable black clothes, and was sitting on a front pew in St Aidan's chapel in Duncrun, halfway up the Binevenagh mountainside, with the view of Magilligan that Dad had described from his last mental wanderings the night before he left for America. The small chapel had filled quickly. Standing room only. From my seat, I couldn't tell whether the attendees were seated according to family – McDermotts to the one side, Finneys to the other. I thought not.

The church service was simple enough, fairly short. Standard funeral fare, I would imagine. References to it being All Saints' Day – a feast day for the hoards of plebeian saints too obscure to have individually assigned days. Mention of requiem services the following day for All Souls'. A bit of organ music from the balcony at the rear. A nice touch, I thought, was that the deacon (as the sole pallbearer of Dad's ashes, which had just arrived from Belfast) placed the urn on a table off-centre from the main aisle – stage left.

While there was no open call for eulogies, I was unexpectedly introduced to the congregation at large and was thus expected to say something fitting. Stalling for ten seconds to collect my thoughts, I thanked everyone for coming. Then I told them, as my voice inevitably broke, that I could do no better than quoting Prince Hamlet when he spoke of his recently departed father:

> He was a man, take him for all in all.
> I shall not look upon his like again.

No, I did not feel hypocritical. I was confused, a thrall to mixed emotions. While I was savouring my father's frequent ghostly visits, I was nonetheless devastated by his death.

When the service ended, Jamie McDermott joined the remainder of the immediate family – myself, Robert,

Robbie, Jane, and, of course, the urn – for a few serious words with the priest. Father Cummings spoke about the long presence of McDermotts in his parish while we settled the modest financial remuneration for the funeral service. From his perspective, I was part of the area's originating community while he was merely a newcomer. It struck me as funny that I, with my few days' presence, embodied Magilligan's oldest blood.

I rode back with the Robert McDermott family to their house. Fiona and Mark Winslow, the cousins-in-law, had gone ahead to greet the others. By the time we arrived, Robbie and Jane's house was overflowing. The two lounges were filled with people, as were the centre hallway, dining room and kitchen. In fact, there were people spilling into the garden from both front and rear doors, in spite of the early November chill.

'You have to understand,' Robbie turned to me, 'this is not typical for us. The old two-day wakes are fading into the past. But the family never all get together anymore, except . . .'

'For weddings and funerals. I know.'

'Usually just funerals these days. And your da's has more of an attraction because of the novelty.'

Jane explained: 'Your father was one of the few who came back after leaving here. He wasn't back long enough to see everyone, so this is the one chance they all have to catch up on news of his life in America. As well as the local gossip.'

It was absolutely amazing to see all these Irish people I'd never met before, together in one place. My family. And they looked like family. I swear I could spot every blood McDermott by sight – dark brown hair, blue eyes, a particular cut of the jaw, the placement of the cheekbones. Some had certain distinct dimples, a light sprinkling of freckles and auburn highlights which shone under direct lighting. The latter characteristics came largely from the lighter-pigmented Finney bloodline and secondarily from outsiders marrying into the family. Some of the Finney brood were blond and there were two or three (I may have counted one cousin twice) redheads.

Robert McDermott senior was tall among the men of his generation. His son Robbie was about the same height as his father and definitely taller than I. I was surprised then that Dad's brother Jamie was relatively short – the runt of the litter, to use an earthy expression. Jamie was more filled out than his brothers, but the look became him, as one who enjoyed good food, good drink and good company. Jamie, now semi-retired, and his wife, Alice, ran a bed-and-breakfast in County Donegal, where their daughter Ellen had remained to look after the house. Jamie's son Harry, close to my age, had taken the day off from the fishery, but his wife and their young son, Tim, had stayed home with colds. Jamie's other offspring were here – Eveline McDermott McNulty and Dennis McDermott with his wife, Mary.

'Tommy,' Jamie greeted me, lightly slapping me on the back. 'You've so much of your da in your mannerisms, I'd know you if I saw you two blocks away in the middle of New York City. I'm Mickey's brother James, if you haven't guessed.'

'Uncle James,' I greeted him.

'Jamie will do.' He quickly turned off his broad smile. 'I'll miss him, your da. We grew up like twins. We were inseparable until we went off to seek our own fortunes, such as they were. Even at that, we both moved west – I across the lough, he across the bigger sea to America.'

I remembered Dad talking about Alice Flaherty, the girl who was the love of Jamie's life in their schooldays, the woman he'd moved across the lough to marry.

Jamie's smile returned. 'We used to fly kites for fun, you know, when we were boys. Mostly sad-looking homemade affairs – crooked twigs, old newspapers, old schoolwork. All pasted together with flour and water into these horrible misshapen, heavy blobs.'

I couldn't help but smile at the picture his words created.

'Oh, but they flew,' he went on. 'We have the breezes here for kite-flying. On the strand was fine, but I liked it better when we took off on a Saturday, hiked up to Binevenagh and flew the kites over the valley. Like we were flying there ourselves, it was . . . Do you hang-glide?'

'Hang-glide?' I repeated, surprised by the change of topic. 'No, why?'

'That's what they do now, from up the mountain. Hang-glide over Magilligan. It's something to see.'

'Really?' was all I could manage in response. I don't know why hang-gliding seemed incongruous to me. Perhaps I thought it a luxury sport, out of keeping with the area's simple life styles.

'You'll come over to our place while you're here,' Jamie continued. 'There's always a room for family.' He added impishly: 'It's called the dungeon.' He must have used that line many times before, but I appreciated his enjoyment in using it once again.

'I will try,' I promised absently and yet sincerely. I hardly knew the man, this uncle, but I liked him instantly.

A woman's voice and figure appeared at his side. 'Enough of that stale "dungeon" joke, Jamie,' she said.

Jamie made the introductions. 'This is Mickey's boy, Tom. My wife, Alice.'

'Ah,' I said, 'the legendary Alice. Dad spoke about you.'

'Did he now?' She was a lovely woman – approachable, with facial features that were generously responsive. She had what is often described as a fresh-scrubbed look. Round, slightly pink cheeks and cartoon-twinkling blue eyes framed by fine wrinkles, pale brown hair lightly touched with grey. Slender, although less so than she must once have been. There was a trace of springiness in her movements, like a dancer traversing a stage. With no disparagement to her present age, I could discern the irresistible young woman who'd sealed Uncle Jamie's future forty-some years earlier. I also understood that Dad must have envied Jamie's fortune.

Young Robbie walked me around the gathering to make introductions to as many of my relatives as possible. I believe I next met the Connors, who were the children and grandchildren of my father's Aunt Maddy, Madeline McDermott Connors, and were from either County Derry or County Antrim, I wasn't sure, or both. Maddy was a bit of a clucking hen, taking all and sundry under her wing. If mothering were what I needed and if it were fifteen or twenty years earlier in time, when Aunt Maddy would have been in her maternal prime, I might have been drawn closer to her. Now Maddy was very old. She confused her grandson Philip with her son Joe, and the granddaughters Polly and Jenny with her daughter-in-law Nancy. I wondered where she placed her great-grandchildren, who weren't present for me to observe. Aunt Maddy's least-muddled thinking and attention were directed towards Brian, her wheelchair-bound husband, whose sparse conversation revealed an absolute clarity of understanding of who was who and what was what.

Father Cummings, blond, short-haired and conservative-looking, approached and offered me a drink of *poitín* ('poteen' in English). As near as I can determine, *poitín* is something of a whiskey, an illegal home brew of varying qualities and assuredly lethal in great quantities. I took a large gulp (my mistake) and sputtered at the raw taste and high alcoholic content.

'My God,' I said, not thinking about the present company, 'where did this come from?'

The priest smirked. 'Best not to ask.' I had to trust that the supplier of this batch had no designs on eliminating the entire McDermott family. Or rendering them blind.

'I wanted to thank you again, Reverend —'

He interrupted. 'Father.'

'Right. Father. Sorry, I'm not exactly adept at religious ... things. Denominations. Titles. The whole vocabulary.'

'All those religious things, yes,' he acknowledged. 'I was surprised that you chose to have a Catholic mass. I was pleased, yes, no mistake. Still, I was surprised, because most of the McDermotts I've encountered never struck me as religious — even those in my parish, I'll admit in private only — and I don't believe I ever saw your father at mass.'

'We're not a particularly religious family, no. As far as I can tell, we're an assortment of the God-fearing and the godless. I'm afraid my own family's the worst. The black sheep, if you will. Certainly heathens. Still, Dad was baptised Catholic and I know he went to church from time to time.'

'Christmas and Easter, I imagine.'

'Not really,' I had to answer honestly. 'He didn't like churches when they were filled with people. He'd rarely go in if there were services going on. Sorry, Rev ... Father.'

He laughed. 'Och. You may as well make it Dan outside the church. I don't believe you'll ever get the hang of the "Father" business. "He'd only go in if there were no services going on,"' he chuckled. 'He was baptised, though, you said. You, as well?'

I shook my head. 'Technically, I was baptised, yes. But it was my mother's doing, for social reasons, and by my reckoning that doesn't count. I mean, I was only a baby. I had no say in the matter, so I don't consider myself bound by the ceremony ... You see, I wasn't exaggerating about being heathens.'

'Heathens, indeed. We'll have to talk about this baptism business another time. And your Anabaptist viewpoint.'

I thought for a moment that I'd offended the considerate Father Dan. But no, he was only leaving me to track down the supply of drink. Before he departed, looking ruefully at his empty glass, he commented in a low voice: 'Some of the most spiritual people I know are dyed-in-the-wool heathens. Don't quote me.'

I was beginning to like this priest. Not terribly officious when the dog collar was off. He didn't have a you'll-come-round-in-the-end-they-all-do attitude. I was still digesting his remarks, along with the *poitín*, when I was accosted by someone who'd surely had too much of the liquor. Unless there were other illegal substances in circulation.

'Shouldn't have come back,' the staggering man slurred at me. 'Go to America, stay there.'

I didn't know whether he was referring to my father or me. Or was he talking about someone else entirely? In any event, he was quite agitated.

'Hello,' I said, extending a hand in friendship. 'I'm Tom . . .'

He spat his words. 'I know who the bloody hell you are. You're the bloody, fucking American. What're you . . .? Why'd you come to . . .?' He was either searching for the right words or holding back a vomit. 'You were born there. Go back. You don't know what . . .' He called on his mental reserves to produce what he must have considered the ultimate insult: 'Fucking Yank!'

'I am an Irish citizen as well,' I said, thinking to appease him.

'You what?'

'I said that I'm an Irish citizen.'

The statement seemed to confound him instead. He swayed a moment, then weaved away into the crowd.

'Are you?' a voice behind me asked. 'Irish, as well?' I turned. The speaker was unquestionably another McDermott, with my colouring and features, and exactly my height.

'As a matter of fact, yes, I am,' I answered. 'Dad had me send in the paperwork years ago, so I am a bona fide dual citizen.'

'Bona fide dual citizen. I like that. That'll be as good a way as any to describe you.' He had a rakish smile, higher on one side. The asymmetry added to his charm.

'That oorie fellow was Andy Rafferty,' he explained. 'Ned's eldest. His grandmother was a McDermott. Andy's on the skids because he's been made redundant – again. Fell out with his wife, Monica. He blames her for getting pregnant and keeping him in this country when he could have emigrated to America, not that he had any particular prospects there. Thinks his younger brother got all the breaks.'

'Did he?' I asked, taking the bait.

'Not a bit. Ned, the second son, went off to London, slaved like a bastard with no time for himself, worked his way up in one company, then transferred to another that brought him back to its Irish offices. Moved back near his parents, married a local woman and now they have a lovely girl, Bobbie, at university in Belfast. She's the only family I know in the city.'

'Which is where you live, I take it?'

'Yes. There except when I'm here.' He extended his hand. 'Walker. McDermott.'

'Of course.' I shook his hand. 'Walker?'

'Umm. Story is I was an error in transcription. Should have been Walter. May only be a story. The longer you associate with this family, the more stories you'll hear. We're second cousins. My father's Everett McDermott – your dad's first cousin. My granddad Colin was your granddad Brendan's brother. My mother's Patricia McMillan McDermott.'

'You do know that most of those names mean nothing to me. I don't have a clue.'

'I know.' He smiled again. He didn't care that I wasn't cowed by his superior knowledge of family relations.

'No O'Somethings in the family?' I wondered.

He thought. 'Curious observation. No, I don't believe so.'

'You said you live here and in Belfast?' I prompted him.

'Quite right. Which is why I need to ask a favour.'

'Ask away.'

'It's about accommodation, you see,' he continued. 'I have a flat in Belfast . . .'

I interrupted. 'Where you . . .'

'I'm an actor.'

'Ah,' I responded, further filling out my understanding of this cousin. In fact, filling in a wealth of information from his profession.

'The folks' home – Coleraine – is still somewhat of a home base. And I would be staying there tonight, but with all the relations from Donegal – the distance and the drinking . . .'

'Yes?' I encouraged.

'None of them want to bother you. Grieving and your being not exactly an outsider but not known well enough to impose on. In a word, mate, can you put me up for the night?'

'Why not? It won't be the first time I provided a flop-house for actors. Of course you can stay. I didn't realise there was problem . . . Is there anyone else who needs . . .?'

'Shh, shh. You may be generous with your living space, but I'm not. No sleeping side-by-side and head-to-foot if I can help it.'

'I know it's a small house,' I said, 'but there were once at least seven people living there. And it was smaller then. At the moment there's only me.'

'You and him,' he said, nodding across the room. I looked and saw my dad's shadow moving towards and out the open back door. 'You've been talking to your father's ghost all along, haven't you?'

'You see him?' I asked. 'Really?'

'Aye, Tom, though not clearly,' he said. 'He's little more than a blur to me, a disturbance in the ether.'

'But how . . .?'

'I believe they call our kind "sensitives".'

'Sensitive? That's you all right, Walker.' The voice came from a dark-blonde-haired woman who'd evidently been listening in. Eavesdropping seemed to be the mode of introduction that evening. 'How do you do?' she said, turning to me.

'Thank goodness,' I said in greeting, 'someone who's neither a McDermott nor clergy. You wouldn't be a Finney cousin, would you?'

'No,' she laughed, 'but you're in the right neighbourhood. I'm not at all related to your lot, but I grew up with some of your Finneys and the Willoughbys, who are also Finneys, so I know all about them. And I live near the Donegal McDermotts.'

'Marnie Dodd,' Walker introduced. 'Tom McDermott.'

'Pleasure,' I said.

She smiled. 'You're another, then? A ghost-seer?'

'I never said that.'

They ignored my weak dissemblance.

'It comes from the Finneys of Donegal, you know,' Walker explained. 'Even though no one talks much about it openly. Fortunately we're New Age children and have no such reservations . . . Your grandmother was a Finney, and her grandfather was Ruairí Finney. They say he was one of the gentry and he couldn't deny it.'

'One of the gentry?' I asked incredulously.

'Not the landed aristocracy,' Walker explained, adding in a stage whisper: 'The fairy folk. The gentle people.'

I considered the implications. 'Wait a minute,' I said to Walker. 'If being descended from a Finney accounts for any supernatural leanings I may have, how do you explain yourself?'

'Did I forget to mention? Your grandmother – Elisabeth? – had a first cousin, Catherine Finney, who lived with Elisabeth's family. They were as thick as thieves. They ended up marrying brothers.'

'Our respective grandfathers, would that be?' I asked.

'None other.'

I thought about the whole explanation before voicing my objections. 'Please don't tell me I'm descended from a leprechaun. I don't like clowns and I rank leprechauns along with them.'

'Leprechauns? No, no leprechauns in the family,' Walker said.

'Nor any in this area at all, I don't believe,' Marnie added. 'I certainly wouldn't know where to look for one.' She was teasing me.

'Except for the soft toys in the tourist shops. What else do you not like about Irish caricatures? After we've tried so hard to make them tourist-friendly.'

'Well,' I laughed, 'I have to admit I was prepared to jump on the next plane back if I was greeted by an old family matron in a linen apron bordered with shamrocks, thumbing rosary beads, wielding a pot of corned beef and cabbage, and wailing "Faith and begorrah, 'tis himself!" Reassure me. Humour me, if you must. It is all propaganda then? Some PR nightmare intended, God only knows why, to cutesify a country torn by famine and politics and . . .? Well, you know the rest.'

'That's the size of it,' said Walker.

'To be fair, though,' Marnie interposed, 'some of what's been romanticised about Ireland is simply what used to be. Like sod houses – picturesque in paintings, but hardly desirable for living in. Anything else that's been bothering you?' she cajoled.

'I don't care for soda bread – not for a proper tea, anyway. I hate parades. I don't wear green. I especially don't drink green beer.'

'Are those requirements in America?' she laughed.

'Absolutely,' I said. 'If you're Irish-American. That's why I'm not terribly good at it.'

'Bah,' said Walker in disgust. 'You won't find that smush here. Any road, not up here in the desolate north. We may cater to the tourist trade as well, but the people live hard and take the local legends serious.'

'None of the stereotypes are true?'

'Well,' admitted Marnie. 'I do know people who are fond of kale. And potatoes are a definite dietary staple. You know where they come from?'

'Potatoes? No.'

'America. The potato came to Europe from South America.'

'Really? Beyond the touristy nonsense then, what does one find here?' I asked. 'For real culture? Besides the theatre.'

'Literature,' Walker answered. 'The Irish, of course, have a superior mastery of the English language – which, I should mention, is what Marnie teaches at school, thus our attraction to each other on a linguistic standing – and the schools in the South have been encouraging everyone to learn Irish . . .'

'And increasingly in the North,' Marnie added.

'Gaelic?' I interrupted.

Walker nodded. 'Irish Gaelic, to be precise. So now we have more of the Irish language appearing in literature, even on the telly.'

'And there's the dancing,' Marnie said, indicating some cousins engaged in what looked to me to be a standard slow dance, certainly not a jig or step-dancing. The family had come prepared to sing and play. A succession of performers was turning the get-together into a wake after all, if not an actual ceilidh.

'Doesn't look traditional to me,' I commented before

thinking. 'But they are light on their feet. Quite elegant.'

'Yes, I believe they won competitions when they were younger. Have you met them?' I shook my head. 'David and Anthea Finney. I was at school with their Connie and Julian.'

'Do you dance?' I asked, then quickly added: 'That is, I'm not asking you . . . I mean, I don't, can't dance.'

'Most of the McDermotts are double-left-footed,' Walker said. 'We're vocal artists instead. Marnie's rather deft as a step-dancer.'

'A generous compliment.'

'But her real talent rests with the fiddle. And it's time for her to show off.'

'Ah, no,' Marnie protested.

'Ah, yes,' Walker insisted. 'Time for both of you, in fact. Everyone does his bit.' He led Marnie away by the hand, and she grabbed mine, dragging me along to the front room.

A POST–FUNERAL CEILIDH

Cousin Dexter Finney was relieved to give up his time in the spotlight with the accordion. He shook out the tension from his fingers then put them to use hefting a glass of beer. The impromptu stage was the area by the piano in the front lounge, towards which I was being reluctantly dragged.

When I dug in my heels and brought the Walker-Marnie-Tom procession to a halt, I felt a touch on my shoulder. I turned to see Robert senior's old, large hand. 'Tommy, Mickey said you've a beautiful voice,' he said. 'What will you sing for him?'

'I ... I don't ... Something traditional?' I offered. I couldn't say no now. 'I do know "Danny Boy," if that's not a cliché?' I expected a look of amused condescension from anyone within earshot. Nothing. 'I only know the first verse and the chorus.'

Walker spoke up. 'I know the second.'

' "Danny Boy" is a perfect choice,' Uncle Robert said. 'It's a local favourite.'

Marnie filled me in. 'The melody was transcribed in the mid-nineteenth century, in Limavady, and the lyrics were added at the turn of the century – by an Englishman, would you believe? An English barrister, who wrote it after he lost his only son. It's said that the tune was a gift from the fairies who played it to a human musician, a blind harpist, while he was sleeping on the banks of the River Roe in Limavady.'

'Hmm,' I responded. 'Those gentle people turn up everywhere, don't they?' As I took a seat at the piano I turned to Marnie, who picked up her instrument from on top of the piano. 'Can you follow if I start?' I asked.

'I'll pick up with an interlude between the verses. Go ahead.'

So I began. A few bars' introduction on the piano. Then I started singing, low so I could reach the high notes later.

> Oh Danny Boy, the pipes, the pipes are calling,
> From glen to glen and down the mountainside.
> The summer's gone and all the roses falling.
> It's you, it's you must go and I must bide.

When I finished the half I knew, Marnie took over for a simple but beautiful interlude. Her 'fiddle' was in fact a rather expensive-looking violin, which she played with skill and definitely in the style of one trained in classical music. I brought the piano back for the second verse and Walker sang the words I didn't know. At best I sang in a modest, cabaret style, suitable for intimate audiences. If he let loose, Walker's controlled, theatre-trained voice could probably reach the back seats in the upper balcony of a concert hall.

As Marnie bent close to whisper in my ear, her hair tickled my cheek. 'Play the first verse again. Sing the chorus.' She somehow instructed Walker as well, because he was silent for the piano-and-violin repeat but came in harmonising with my voice on the first chorus:

> But come ye back when summer's in the meadow,
> Or when the valley's hushed and white with snow.
> It's I'll be here, in sunshine or in shadow.
> Oh, Danny Boy. Oh, Danny Boy, I love you so.

There was a misting in Uncle Robert's eyes, I saw, when we stopped. He'd been sitting nearby, but he rose now with the aid of a well-used stick. 'That was fine, Tom,' he spoke softly. 'You go on a while yet. I'll be listening.' With that, he stepped outside, where, through open windows, he could still hear the talking, and the music and singing rolling into the darkening sky. And if he was misty-eyed, he could blame the moist night air.

I watched him, illuminated from the lights of the house, walk over to an evergreen tree where he lit a cigarette and seemed to be speaking. I couldn't quite make out what he was saying – something about brimstone? Then he stooped to pet a dog half-hidden in the shadows.

While deciding what to play next, my mind turned to the task ahead of me – stealing away to the strand to set my father's ashes free – and I began to play the 'Skye Boat Song'. ('Loud the winds howl, loud the waves roar, thunder claps rend the air. / Baffled our foes stand by the shore. Follow they do not dare.') Then I decided to take a break before I found myself launching into 'Loch Lomond'. While I was refilling my glass of *poitín* – only my second – I noticed that I'd led Marnie astray into my inexplicable Scottish trend. She was playing an instrumental version of 'Laddie Lie Near Me', accompanied by yet another unknown cousin, with a flute.

'Should I play something else?' I asked Walker. 'Or can I gracefully bow out, having done my duty?'

'I think you're off the hook. The talent pool's at high tide tonight.' He frowned. 'But if anyone should press the issue, you don't know any country music. American country, that is.'

'Why's that? I do know one or two country tunes,' I offered, trying to be helpful.

He shot me a murderous look. 'No you don't,' he hissed. 'Not one bloody country-and-western song. Got it?'

'Sure.' I shrugged. My forte is folk blues anyway, not country. I might have recalled some Woody Guthrie songs if pressed. The truth is that, to my surprise, I enjoyed performing and was invigorated by the experience. Another night, perhaps – under quieter circumstances. Besides, entertaining was not my primary purpose here. And, as Walker noted, there were a remarkable number of others well qualified to perform.

Marnie's violin rendition of 'The Tennessee Waltz', accompanied by another pianist, was a choice that pleased cousins David and Anthea, and the other dancers. When she excused herself for a break, Marnie's place was taken by the flautist, who played two solitary, sad tunes and disappeared, to be replaced by another willing musician, a woman singing unaccompanied mouth music – locally called lilting. She was singing some sort of lament, in what must have been Irish.

Dad never mentioned that every single individual in his family seemed to be musically inclined. Perhaps, I speculated, it's something in the air, something in the water of these northernmost counties of the island.

Some half-hour later, true to Walker's fears, the music was headed towards hardcore country-and-western ground. It seemed a good time to plan our exit.

After rounds of goodbyes and repeated condolences (during which Aunt Maddy apologised for her nephew Andy Rafferty's rudeness and explained that he'd been in bad straits ever since the day he ploughed under what was said to be a fairy grove in his field, and Maddy's husband,

Brian, corrected her that it was a neighbour from her childhood, not Andy, that that had happened to), we drove our three cars – mine, Walker's and Marnie's – down to my house. The families would surely forgive my early departure – as a relative stranger among them and as the only son of the deceased. Nor would they reproach Walker and Marnie for following to see me safely home.

'Nice job of remodelling,' Marnie commented when we were inside.

'Dad's doing. All the modern conveniences.'

She was drawn to the photos scattered about the living room. 'You, of course,' she commented, referring to an eight-by-ten glossy.

'Job requirement,' I said. 'The all-important professional headshot.'

Walker held up a framed photo. 'A boy and his dog?' It was me again, in my early college years, with a big, floppy-eared, brown dog.

'Dad's dog. Woody. A great old mutt. He was already full-grown when Dad got him. If he was a one-man dog, he must have been waiting all his life to meet my father. He loved the woods – that's how Dad named him, obviously.'

'That is precisely the kind of casual photo I like,' said Marnie, admiring the shot. Who could blame her? Woody was one fine-looking dog.

'Who's this?' Walker asked, moving on.

I looked at the only picture of Mom that Dad kept. 'My parents. Before they were married.' I anticipated the next questions as they moved on down the line of furniture. 'And this is my stepsister, Sharon, with her family. Then Dad and two of his brothers before he emigrated; there's a better picture in the bedroom. These are some more relatives, I believe.'

'That's Great Aunt Maddy!' shouted Walker, picking up the old photo.

'Is it?'

'Maddy, and her sisters May and Hannah. May died young. Hannah married a Rafferty; Andy, Ned and Ellen are her grandchildren. The boy is my granda, Colin McDermott.'

'Whose wedding picture?' Marnie asked. It was not a commercial photo of a couple in front of a church, but was a blurred grey shot of a man and woman by an old farm house, possibly the Robert/Robbie McDermott residence in an earlier generation.

'My grandparents, Brendan McDermott and Elisabeth Finney McDermott.'

Marnie commented: 'I've met your grandmother. And your grandfather, I believe, at Robbie and Jane's wedding. You were there as well, Walker.'

'Odd,' I observed. 'They were my grandparents. I never met them, but you both did.'

'And lastly,' Walker said, picking up an ancient daguerreotype appropriately set in a heavy metal frame, 'the father of them all, and our great-grandfather, as a young man – Duncan McDermott. God knows where he had this picture taken. Or when.' The where was probably Derry, because the family didn't travel far afield. The greater mystery was why the photo existed, since it must have been quite an extravagance at the time. 'My lot have a copy of this photo in Coleraine. The frame's not as nice as this.'

'Very impressive,' said Marnie. 'I would think it's bad enough being surrounded by family out there, let alone having four generations watching your every move from these photos.'

'I hadn't thought of it that way,' I laughed. 'Still, I'm not easily spooked.'

'That's fortunate,' Walker remarked absently.

The remaining tour of the house consumed five minutes at most. Then we settled into the study, where I'd started a slow-burning turf fire. I was looking at the urn of ashes I'd set on the piano.

'You play the violin beautifully,' I said to Marnie. 'Have you performed professionally?'

'I only play for my own amusement,' she said.

'And at your school,' Walker added.

'And at my school.' She tried shifting my attention. 'You do quite well yourself on the piano. You should have played longer.'

'No,' I laughed. 'It's just as well I stopped when I did. Somehow I got into Scottish tunes and was getting in deeper by the minute. I might have launched into "Scotland the Brave"!'

'Ah, but do you know the words?' Walker asked.

I cleared my throat and began to sing *a cappella* and as boldly as I'd learned the song:

> Hark when the night is falling.
> Hear, hear, the pipes are calling,
> Loudly and proudly calling down through the glen.
> There where the hills are sleeping
> Now feel the blood a-leaping
> High as the spirits of the old Highland men.

I stopped. 'Believe me now?'

'And how is it that you know "Scotland the Brave"?' Walker asked. 'You didn't learn that from your father, did you?'

I shook my head. 'You know who Artemis Grant is?'

'The Scottish opera singer?' He raised an eyebrow in scepticism. 'Don't tell me you interviewed Artemis Grant and he took you on as his protégé.'

'Not at all. He was already well known by then. I happened to run into him in a pub outside Inverness.' I waved away the question Walker was about to ask. 'How I came to be there is a long, complicated story involving fog in

Oslo. Anyway, we became drinking buddies and he taught me a number of Scottish ballads.'

My attention turned back to my father's urn. 'By the way,' I asked, as casually as I could, 'would either of you know where I could hire a boat?'

They looked at me and at the urn.

'Planning a side trip back to Inverness?' Walker asked facetiously. 'You're on the wrong side of Scotland, you know.'

Marnie ignored his sarcasm. 'You're not likely to find anything on this side of the lough,' she said. 'I may be able to arrange something for Sunday, if you come over to Greencastle. For the day?'

'I could stay over for Sunday, as well, if you need an able-bodied actor's sea hands,' Walker volunteered. Looking at Marnie, then me, he added: 'Or not. As the case may be.'

It was almost a plan. I was the one to thwart it. 'I'm going over to London Sunday morning. Looks like it'll have to wait until I return.'

Marnie sounded disappointed. 'If you're still here the following weekend ...' she proposed with no obvious expectations.

So we left the ash disposal project at that. I didn't relish the possibility of leaving the task unfinished indefinitely, but I couldn't do anything at present. I might give Marnie a call when I was back from London, to put me in contact with someone to hire a boat. I'd prefer undertaking my ocean-bound escapade in her company, but she'd be tied up with teaching during the week. As for the weekend ... I expected to return to the States long before the weekend.

9

MARNIE AND WALKER

In the meantime, we were getting along splendidly – Marnie and I, Walker and I, all three of us. By and by we stumbled onto politics – an inevitable subject for a visitor in a divided country, my fatherland.

'I defer to Marnie as the expert in political matters,' Walker begged off. 'I confess that I am merely an actor totally immersed in the artistic world and ignorant of current affairs. Except as they play on stage.' He tended to play an actor, I saw, when it suited his purposes.

'Bollocks,' I responded, not unkindly.

I addressed Marnie instead. 'Perhaps then you could explain things to me. For one, I don't understand the position of the British in Northern Ireland. Are they accepted or does everyone want to drive them out?'

'It's not that simple,' she said. 'It's not unlike your American Civil War in some ways.'

Walker added: 'Or like the American Revolution.'

Marnie continued. 'Even in the same family, you can find a range of viewpoints. You see, you can be born here in the North and consider yourself Irish or British or both. Either way, you might have centuries of roots on this island. And even if you hold yourself out as Irish, that doesn't rule out being a unionist.'

' "Unionist" meaning?'

'A unionist or loyalist supports keeping Northern Ireland as part of the United Kingdom – that is, in continued union with Britain. A republican advocates that the northern counties be reunited with the Republic of Ireland.'

Again Walker, reputedly apolitical, spoke up. 'You see, despite their feeling a national ethnic identity, an Irishness if you will, some people feel that Northern Ireland is best served by British administration.'

'On the other hand,' Marnie added, 'Northern Ireland is, at best, an unnatural entity. Although the British government supplies important services to the North which some say the Republic could not afford to provide – the pension scheme, for example – others argue that the greatest expenditures are for the military forces required to enforce British control.'

'I take it, then,' I said, 'that the reunification issue does not necessarily run along religious lines.'

'My opinion,' said Walker, 'is that the religious conflicts are driven by history to some extent but primarily by politics.'

Marnie continued. 'As you say, reunification is far from being a clearcut issue. The dozen or so political parties elected within the North alone reflect the dichotomy – some for reunification with the Republic, others for retained union with the UK.'

I was beginning to understand. Mostly I was understanding that this can of worms was beyond one night's comprehension.

'And the name "Ulster",' I said, 'indicates Northern Ireland, the UK domain, that is?'

Walker only laughed at me and shook his head. 'You didn't really think it would be as simple as that, did you?'

Marnie sighed and began to explain as to a child (which, in terms of Ireland's government and politics, I was). 'Historically, Ireland is comprised of four provinces, which each contain a number of counties. The provinces are Connacht, Ulster, Munster and Leinster. Ulster has nine counties – six in the North, three in the South. "Ulster" is probably used more within the North than elsewhere, despite its geographic imprecision. And I should explain that the term "Southern Ireland" can be offensive to people in the South, the Republic. As is the term "Éire" when used by the British. But in the north – the broadly geographical north, that is – the designations of "North" and "South" are commonplace, with no ulterior connotation – most of the time – to distinguish between the political entities of Northern Ireland and the Republic of Ireland.'

'Of course,' Walker added, 'we do end up with the odd circumstance of County Donegal, which is northernmost of any county in Ireland, technically being in the "South".'

'There is that,' Marnie agreed.

Eventually Marnie had to leave to chauffeur some of my cousins back home across the lough; she was the designated, non-drinking driver. I saw her outside to her car. The air was wet with mist and permeated by the aroma of home fires. Beyond the orange lights of the prison the western sky bore a faint pink glow – lights in County Donegal. Greencastle, Marnie said, the site of a revived fishing industry.

Our goodbyes were unexpectedly awkward. I promised to let her know if I'd be coming over to Donegal. We didn't shake hands, didn't kiss. We shivered, in shirt sleeves, lingering by her car. Finally, Marnie said it was nice meeting me, then she drove away and I went inside.

I didn't realise I'd sighed aloud until Walker commented on it. 'Yeah, I know. She's a wild sonsy lass. It's a pity to let her go.'

'Oh?' I asked. 'Did you have certain intentions toward Ms Dodd?'

'Me? No. I'm taken at the moment.' He sat down in what I'd taken to thinking of as Dad's chair. While I was outside he'd found a couple of glasses and poured out some *poitín* from a bottle he'd procured at Robbie's. He gave me a glass. 'Besides, Marnie's too much of a homebody for me ... I say that in admiration. She has her feet firmly planted in this soil. She's not one to travel the world chasing some elusive dream.'

'Yes,' I agreed, 'it is a pity.' I was far too smart to ask myself exactly what I meant by that. I liked her, I'd admit that much. I liked being with her. The few hours we'd shared were not adversarial, as male–female romantic encounters tend to be. Were more intimate relations inevitable or precluded?

'On our lone at last,' Walker sighed, toeing off his shoes, stretching out along the sofa. 'Not that I mind Marnie. Actually, I ... She's nearly family. Well, perhaps not like family after all. Only family know you well enough to accept you with all your faults. They have to.'

'So she doesn't accept your faults? Is that what you're saying?'

He didn't answer. He only held out his glass for me to refill.

'At this point,' I said, 'I probably know Marnie a bit better than I know you.'

'Umm,' he agreed, not taking the bait. 'Lovely lass, isn't she?' Then he added: 'I can say I know you rather well. I met your dad. He spoke about you. And I've read your magazine. Nice work. Literate, even.'

'Thanks,' I said, acknowledging the compliment. 'Conversely,' I said, pushing my point, 'I haven't seen your work at all.'

'You will,' he answered confidently.

'And I know very little about you, other than that your parents are Patricia and ... Everett? – and that you were accidently named Walker. I did meet them tonight, didn't I?'

'Mum was a dancer,' he said, 'but she didn't keep up with it after she married Da. He was, is a teacher. Like our Marnie. At university in Coleraine. I was an indifferent student there myself. Bored, mostly.'

'Were you a class clown then?'

'Not at all. Comedy's not my ... what's the word?'

'Shtick?'

'Thank you, yes. Comedy's not my shtick. No, I simply didn't get much out of the classroom experience as such, although I suppose I acquired some yen for learning from Da, in spite of myself. And some element of the theatrical, if little dancing ability, from Mum.' He smiled broadly. 'And my incomparably handsome looks came from refinement of the best features of the generations that have gone before. And you? Not the looks; they're obvious.'

'Music from Dad, of course. And the writing?' I'd never had to consider the source of my talents before. I shrugged. 'Both my parents were well educated. I suppose my mother did put a lot of emphasis on speaking well, on being grammatically correct and socially proper. Dad tempered that approach with the attitude that there's an appropriate time for everything. He stressed a diverse education. It might seem strange that he never emphasised my Irish roots – or his own. I understand, though, that it's always been important for immigrants to lose their ethnic distinctions and assimilate as quickly as possible into American culture. Odd, isn't it, for a society that prides itself on being a melting pot?'

'As long as everyone melts into the dominant culture.' He yawned.

The yawn was appropriate. It was getting late and I too was wearing down. Let the old-timers keep the party going at Robbie's. I was tired.

'Tired?' I asked.

'Exhausted. Not that I'm not up to being pleasant to family, no matter how great the strain. It's just been a lengthy performance tonight. Give us a hand up, would you?'

He raised a lazy arm half-heartedly. I grabbed it and dragged him to his feet.

'No act for you, though,' he added. 'Or Marnie. I'm too comfortable with you guys to bother being on best behaviour.' He yawned again. 'Where am I sleeping?'

I led him to the guest room and left him undressing before an imminent collapse into bed.

'Goodnight,' he said. 'I'm fair knackered. I won't even bother to dream tonight.'

''Night, Walker,' I said. I expected I'd also drop into a long sleep too deep for any dreaming.

Somnus brevis I

ONE OF THE GOOD PEOPLE

Some dreams are illusory – settings changing from moment to moment, faces morphing one into another. Some dreams are tangible – sharp, crisper than reality, as colourful as a cinematographic glamorisation of mundane events.

One dream that night, in the realistically preternatural category, survived into waking consciousness. It began with me as an observer, standing on the back slope of a hill. The green of the surrounding lawn and trees was vivid and crisp. The sky's graphic dark clouds promised an eventual harmless rain. To my left was a rough stone cottage, intruding halfway into the hillside. The outer door was ajar; the interior dark. From the door, the hill sloped gently to a tiny cove – a sheltered, calm inlet leading beyond my range of vision and, I somehow knew, eventually into a salty harbour and the ocean at large. But here, where the water was shallow and fresh, a beached rowboat could be gently coaxed out onto a motionless lough.

A young man, in his early or mid-twenties, was loading such a rowboat with fishing gear. His eyes were brilliant blue. His hair was a thatch of dark red curls falling over his forehead, shorter at the sides, partially covering his ears and neck. He wore breeches and a loose, pleated shirt that was a yellow faded near-white. In some ways, he could have fitted into the world of the 1990s. And yet ... As those thoughts crossed my mind, I knew he was looking back at me from the year 1622. And I knew he was part of my heritage, my genetic make-up – I sensed that he was some sort of an ancestor.

'Beautiful land,' I commented, referring to the green expanses around us.

'This is the oxter of Ireland,' he said. I didn't know then that 'oxter' means 'armpit', but the sentiment was clear. I felt the misery behind his words.

'Here? But it's ...'

'You don't know what it's like,' he said, countering my observation of the obvious lushness of his physical environs. His youthful existence lacked fulfilment. He saw ahead of him desolation, a hard life with no rewards, no prospects but work and death.

'You don't know what lies ahead,' I responded. I could only hope to assure him that the apparent lack of opportunity did not preclude any future happiness in his life. Even without happiness, he might be content in the knowledge that, long after his death, his offspring would for some time enjoy the benefits of the sea and of the land he now cavalierly possessed. And, far beyond the young red-haired man's future, his progeny might embrace the wealth of his existence passed down through generations. How could I, Tom, ever expect to translate my perceptions to his present frame of mind?

I couldn't. I could only look on him and ache for an impossible, subliminal connection. Or was I somehow, on that subconsciousness level, already communicating a message of hope? Did he recognise in me a distant, positive reflection of his life? Because I saw that look – the look of a young man cursed with no future, caught in despair and even on the brink of suicide – disappear. His brow smoothed. The frown lifted.

'Come,' he said. He motioned me to the old boat. 'Do you fish?'

'No,' I responded, taking the hand he offered to help me on board. Touching his hand was much like touching my dead dad's hand; he shouldn't have felt like a living being, yet he did.

'What is your name?' I asked.

'Call me John, if you like,' he said with humour. 'John Silver.'

'I don't think so,' I said. 'John Silver – Long John Silver, the pirate – won't be written about for another two hundred and fifty years. In fiction.'

'Seán, then,' he said cheerfully. It seemed that I'd passed some test by seeing through the false name. 'That's the truth of it. Of the family called Finney.'

'Tom,' I responded. 'Thomas *Sean* McDermott.'

He stared hard at me, but he accepted that my middle name was truly Sean and I was not humouring him.

'John is, of course, Seán,' I continued, working out his joke as I was talking. 'And Silver?'

'Sylvanus,' he muttered. 'An old name in the family.' He would not elaborate, so I did.

'Not the human side of the family, obviously. Sylvanus – god of fields and forests. An ancestor from the other side? One of the good people? An ancestor of hundreds, perhaps thousands of years past? . . . The god Sylvanus specialised in husbandry, not fishing.'

His look was cautious.

'What do you know of it?' he asked.

'I know that elfin blood runs in my Finney line.'

'Elfin? Yes, that's one of the words others use. Our talents, our skills cover many areas. Farming and breeding, yes. More of us, my family, have turned to the sea in these times. Or perhaps we've *re*turned to the sea, I don't know, our people are so old I can't fathom it all myself.'

'Your people? Is that why you're unhappy? Because of the deal that the fairy folk made? The deal that keeps them underground – which is, I take it, more of a figurative term than geographic.' I noted that his cottage, which was not exactly underground, might well be hidden from sight to someone on the road.

His response was refreshingly unguarded. 'There was a pact long ago when co-existence of our kind with human people seemed, at best, unworkable. The "good people" as you've said, the fairy folk, decided to assume a primarily non-visible presence.'

'Decided or agreed?'

'Does it matter?'

I shrugged.

'At the end of the day,' he continued, 'it proved a difficult arrangement. More difficult, though, has been the commingling of the two cultures.'

'Cross-breeding, you mean?'

'Are you the expert in husbandry then?' he retaliated.

I smiled. 'Not at all,' I answered, as he calmly took oars in hand to row us out into the isolated lough. ' "Miscegenation" was the term once used in America; it was a concept feared by small-minded people … Has your bloodline commingled already? Were you born … on the other side?'

'Both my parents were born of the gentry,' he said. 'So was I.' He hesitated before adding: 'I had a grandfather who was human.'

'And you are the confused offspring – generations

removed from an ethnically clear lineage, one way or the other. You feel that you're a misfit in the world of your adult existence? You don't know what to make of it all? Is that the size of it?'

He did not answer. At length, as he stopped rowing, our boat came to rest over deep waters near the centre of the bay. He prepped a pole with fishing line, and dropped an unbaited hook into the sea.

'Seán?' I ventured. 'Seán Sylvanus. Also of the Finney line?'

'Yes,' he responded, as he immediately reeled in a thrashing, silvery sea trout, 'Thomas Sean McDermott. More questions?'

As I took a moment to gather my thoughts, I was again drawn in to the striking, cinematic aspects of the scene. It didn't matter that I knew it was a dream.

'Somehow . . .' I began. 'Somehow I know, as surely as you are aware, that your parents survived the mixture of cultures, being predominantly gentry in the humans' world. I don't know how life will turn out for you or what your future will be. I don't know whether you can manage life in the human world. That is, I don't know for certain, although' – I hesitated, not knowing how I'd obtained these incredible insights – 'I do have reason to believe you'll do fine.'

Having successfully netted another catch, he stopped his work to look at me. 'You're only a figure in my dream. How would you know anything?'

'I know,' I responded, 'that *you're* a player in *my* dream. Nonetheless, I believe you're real. You may as well assume I'm also real. And I know that one of your descendants, some thirteen generations from now, will marry a human by the name of Brendan McDermott – my grandfather.'

He hesitated. 'There is much that the human world has learned from us, including our music and our dance. They have never learned how to enter our thoughts.'

'Who but the offspring of gentry could possibly have that ability?'

'Can the bloodline be maintained that far?' he wondered, surely with doubt. 'So many generations.'

I responded by dipping my hand into the water and, with a flick of my fingers, signalling a good-sized salmon to swim into my grasp. As I swooped the pinkish fish into the boat, I said: 'Question answered?'

10

WALKIES

Late the next morning I awoke to the last heavy drops of the night's rain, falling like phantom footsteps in the yard. I hadn't had much more *poitín* last night after we left Robbie's but I still felt the need to purge my head of sleep.

In the smaller bedroom, my cousin Walker was still asleep, although he stirred from time to time.

'Wake up already,' I greeted him.

'Go away,' he responded, not opening his eyes. Then he mumbled: 'What time is it?'

'Quarter after ten.'

He moaned, rubbing and opening his eyes, clearly unwilling to sit up. 'I need a clean shirt,' he grumbled.

'Not until after you've showered.'

'I need a cup of coffee.'

'You can have breakfast after we get back.'

'Get back from where?'

'Walkies. Out to the Point and back. We need fresh air to

clear out the cobwebs.'

He moaned again. 'I have a better idea. You go for walkies, I'll sleep.'

'That's all right,' I said. 'I'll wait.' I pulled up a chair, sat and propped my feet on the bed.

Walker dropped off for a few minutes, then stirred again, turned away from me and turned back. 'Stop it!' he yelled. 'I can't sleep with you watching me.'

'I wasn't. I was day-dreaming.'

'I've decided I hate you after all,' he responded. He slowly sat up, on the edge of the bed, and began to pull on yesterday's clothes. 'Is it cold out?'

'You've got a sweater.' Finally I relented. 'I'll make coffee to take along.' I went out to the kitchen, trusting that he would not crawl back under the covers.

Ten minutes later we were outside, already sipping at the thermal flask of fresh, steaming coffee. A ground fog was hovering up to knee level. The sun hadn't broken through, but the broad field of grey clouds was broken here and there. I saw the potential for decent weather ahead.

As we headed towards the Point, we passed the unavoidable British Army barracks and were overtaken by a jogging troop of soldiers returning to the fortification. Their leader nodded greeting in passing. They seemed to be, and I'm certain they were, regular people – the kind of blokes you'd meet in the local pub. I hoped, perhaps naively, that their mission here did not run counter to the lives of the locals.

'Do you know any of them?' I asked Walker.

'Not by name. I've met a few hereabouts,' he commented. No rancour. Insouciance.

We didn't speak again until we reached the Point. The broad view was still obscured by mist; the sand and grasses were wet. Conversation over shared coffee was light (very light) and brief. My thoughts were on the ocean, my father's ashes and visiting my cousins and Marnie in Donegal. Whatever Walker's thoughts were, he kept them to himself.

We were in Derry by early afternoon. Walker criticised the road I'd taken, through the centre of Limavady, and promised to navigate our return. I'd begun to rely on the A2 route as my lifeline, so I'd assumed it was the route of choice. Not so, said Walker. Trust him for guidance through his native land.

When we were well beyond Limavady, he directed me across the River Foyle, down along the Strand Road, and into a modern, multi-storey car park adjacent to the old city of Derry. Now on foot, we climbed the stairs for a panoramic walk along the top of the city walls. We looked down the hillside, towards the river. Walker described the lay of Derry outside the walls and beyond our limited lines of vision – the different sections on either side of the water. He talked about the area's commercial enterprises and told me that the city at large showed promise for a burgeoning computer industry. Really? I thought to myself. The potential for a future *Heights* article implanted itself in my mind.

We turned then to the city of Derry itself – the old city encompassed within the walls. Walker led us down along Artillery Street to point out the Playhouse, and farther along, on Market Street, the Rialto, at both of which he had performed. Midway between the two theatres we stopped, stood over the Ferry Quay Gate for a view of the two-block length of street from the gate to the Diamond in the centre. Within the walls, the streets were narrow, two-cars' width, with two-, three- and four-storey buildings on either side. A sizeable portion of the city had been rebuilt after extensive destruction during the violence of the troubles in the 1970s. Many restored buildings that should have been old now looked new. It was a pleasant and presently peaceful city in all, and I had to remind myself that the cease-fire was not of long standing and remained tentative. I remembered visits to London, when underground stations, commercial buildings and so on were subjected to IRA (and more recently Real IRA) bombs.

Walker pointed out the gothic St Columb's Cathedral – a strife-damaged and rebuilt cathedral that displayed a curious hollow cannonball, which had been lobbed into the walled city during the siege of 1688–9 and contained the terms of surrender – which were refused by the city's residents. I had to admire a people who memorialised their resistance.

Near Bishop's Gate, I began to see indisputable evidence of the city's more recent troubles. The city's RUC police station and army post were enshrouded in tall walls and metal fences – even metal fences surrounding the high-windowed walls of an observation tower. A tall metal-latticed tower held spotlights and video-cameras, aimed towards a valley which once, long ago, was the bed of a fork in the River Foyle that isolated the city as an island.

'That,' said Walker, indicating the neighbourhood below us, 'is the Bogside.' Walker told me about the violence and outrages that took place in near history, when he and I were about eight or nine. The Bogside is a distinctly Catholic and nationalist neighbourhood, home of the 'Free Derry' movement. During a civil rights march on the thirtieth of January 1972, the British Army opened fire on the unarmed protesters, shooting thirteen men dead and fatally wounding another. Neither the soldiers who killed the civilians nor the officers who gave the command to shoot were disciplined. The atrocity has come to be called Bloody Sunday. From the height of the city walls, I could see graphic commemorations of the past violence and continuing unrest. A couple of murals read 'NO CONSENT NO PARADE' and the balcony walls of a two-building apartment complex spelled out 'NO SECTARIAN MARCHES' – a reference to the open hostility against Protestant Orange Order marches through Catholic nationalist neighbourhoods. There were other wall paintings depicting conflicts and referencing by year events I couldn't identify. The signs of violence, the reminders, were over-whelming. And yet, just a few yards farther along, within the city walls was nestled the quiet church and churchyard of St Augustine's – serene and isolated from the symbols and trappings of violence. And a mural on the wall of a nearby youth hostel advocated peaceful cohabitation of different cultures.

We descended the city walls at Butcher Gate and walked up Magazine Street to the Apprentice Boys' Hall. In the early seventeenth century, Walker explained, James I of England, James Stuart, instituted the planting of Protestant Scottish and English colonists into the province of Ulster, which dispossessed the native Irish Catholic landholders. It was the plantation policy that brought wealthy English Protestant merchants into Londonderry. When native Irish rebelled throughout the county, in the mid-century, the city of Londonderry resisted their attack. By then the English crown had been taken from Catholic James II and given to William III of Orange and his wife Mary, James II's Protestant daughter. James II fled to France then to Ireland, where, in a plan to use his French and Irish troops to regain the English throne, he marched to Derry. However, the city's citizens feared massacre and thirteen apprentices locked the Ferry Gate against James's garrison, and so began the siege of Derry, broken after three months by the arrival of Williamite relief forces.

'A-level in history?' I asked Walker in response to this flood of information. He laughed. While the details of his historical summary left me confused, I was beginning to understand the conflict between the names 'Derry' and

'Londonderry' – as graphically demonstrated in official signs where the 'London' portion was spray-painted out.

Next to the hall, behind an iron fence, stood a damaged, larger-than-life-size statute.

'Not my namesake,' Walker explained. 'He's the Reverend George Walker, a leader in the 1689 resistance. He also recorded the events.'

We stopped for pints on Shipquay Street, where the Glue Pot Bar held claim to being the oldest public house in Derry, having been established in 1684. Over our drinks, in response to my queries, Walker elaborated on his theatrical training in Derry, giving dates and names of productions. I was beginning to learn more about the modern Irish theatre and about my cousin's world.

After checking out the Tower Museum and the Craft Village nestled within the middle of a city block, we left the inner city and passed by the Guildhall, which was both interesting architecturally and demoralising historically as (according to Walker) the seat of government-sanctioned discriminatory policies. Nearby, in Waterloo Place, there stood statues of an emigrating family. The whole of the area struck me first as somewhat depressing, in light of the old and ongoing troubles and the volume of emigration the city had witnessed. On the other hand, Derry was ever hopeful. As in the multitude of European cities that suffered through centuries of wars, Derry's everyday life always re-emerged and the economy was again on the uprise.

As we worked our way back to the car, I stopped woolgathering long enough to remember a vital errand. I dragged Walker into the Foyleside shopping mall to visit the Marks & Spencer department store.

'Shopping?' he asked, not terribly pleased at the prospect.

'You're wearing my last clean shirt,' I reminded him.

Just short of entering Limavady on our return, Walker

instructed me to turn off the A2 proper and onto a road bypassing the town and rambling into the countryside.

'What is this road?' I asked.

'This is the B69,' he answered. 'It's the Seacoast Road.'

'The Seacoast Road? I thought the A2 was the Seacoast Road.'

'It is,' he said. 'Somewhere after you turn off Murderhole Road. This route goes through Myroe.'

'Oh,' I responded. No wonder Inspector Tennent had led me personally to Dad's house instead of giving me directions.

I immediately saw the visual attraction of the alternate route. Instead of multiple turns and winding along the base of hills, this road opens onto a wide perspective of flat, broad fields barely above sea level (and sometimes below, I understand) – a fertile plain reclaimed from Lough Foyle. Then suddenly, as the road approaches a little bridge over the River Roe before it rejoins the A2, there appears an irresistible photo op – a photographically opportune view of Binevenagh, looming at four hundred metres like a private mountain over the Magilligan valley. The vista is stark and devastatingly beautiful, like a blizzard or a hurricane welcoming any stranger willing to suffer its brutal indifference. This new Old World was beginning to grow on me.

The rural northern expanse of the county struck me intensely, like a heavy thump deep in the chest. In the city of Derry, within the old walls, I felt a sense of history in general all around me. Here, among the plain, the fields, the looming mountain and the timeless strand of Magilligan, I experienced an awareness of personal history. I'd been enraptured by the spirits of the soil and the air.

I cooked dinner myself that night – salmon, which abounds in the North. Again I was very conscious of the oven and everything around me being 'my things' – more than mere possessions, they were items of comfort. And the oven even broiled the salmon with a wonderfully even heat.

After dinner, before retiring, we spent some time in a conveniently close pub. I was already recognised there as 'the American'.

'Say,' I addressed Walker as we were walking back to the house, 'you know something about language, don't you?'

'A bit. Why?'

'I've always wondered ... Actually, I suppose it's a prejudice. I've never understood the difficulty with pronouncing *th* as *t* in Irish-American communities. You know, the stereotypical tirty-tird for thirty-third. Does that come from a regional Irish dialect? I don't notice the problem around here.'

'No, you wouldn't here. It's not exactly a regional trait though,' he answered. 'It comes from the Irish language itself. You see, there is no equivalent to the English *th* sound in Irish. The *th* sounds, I should say, because there are two.'

Putting to use his study of dialects (and tossing out impressive words like 'labio-dental' and 'fricative'), Walker explained that the *th* called *edh* or *eth* – as in 'the' – generally turned into a *d* sound for Irish-speakers learning English, and was passed on that way to their descendants. The other *th*, the thorn – as in the word 'three' – became *t*. So, 'this thing' might be pronounced by a *th*-deficient Irish individual as 'dis ting'. In contrast, he elaborated, the thorn became *f* in Cockney English.

'And that trend seems to be growing,' I commented.

'Yes,' he agreed. 'You'll hear "fing" for "thing" not just on *Eastenders* these days, but in Oxford and Cambridge as well.'

'So it's not evidence of lack of education,' I concluded.

'Not at all. Although it's only natural that, since one tends to assimilate the speech characteristics of one's environment, a lengthy life in English academia would tend to produce the *th* sound you're used to ... Don't you like the Irish accents?'

'I don't know ... I suppose I find the *f* substitute for *th* less objectionable than the *t* sound.'

'You're a cultural snob!' he accused me – with good humour, of course.

'If I am, I apologise. It could just be a matter of what I'm used to.'

'Hmm. Well, there's somefing to tink about.'

'Ha ha.'

We had reached my little bungalow, with a welcoming light glowing in the kitchen. The house was still warm inside and dry against the misty night.

'I did notice,' I went on, 'that some of the people in Derry – the city, I mean – were very hard to understand. Would they be from somewhere in the South? Like that bloke in the pub?'

'Him? No, that was a Derry dialect. I couldn't tell which neighbourhood.'

'It was a strong accent though, wasn't it? It's not just me.'

'Aye, his dialect was rather thick. There is more of an Irish flavour to their speech in Derry. And there's the slang. It's harder to make out what people are saying when you're not familiar with the expressions.'

Good point. 'Tea or ...?'

'I'll take "or".'

I poured us a couple of whiskies.

'How do you find the local dialect, around here?' Walker was asking.

'It's growing on me,' I answered. 'I'm starting to tune into it more. The younger people are easier for me to understand.'

He nodded. 'Hmm. They're more Anglicised. More worldly, to be sure.'

'And,' I continued, for the first time realising what I must have picked up on some time ago, 'there's a Scottish sound to the language up here.'

'That's right. Northern Ulster is what some call the dialect – part of the highly regionalised "Norn Iron" language. There are strong cultural and historical ties between the northern coast and Scotland. Clever of you to pick that up.'

That was a relief. I should get by much better if I remembered to put on my Scottish ears when I was out and about in the borough.

We had settled by the turf-burning hearth in the study. Now there was an apparent discrepancy. For as comfortable as I was in every corner of this memory-saturated family abode, I had immediately staked out the study – an entirely new room – as my centre of operations. Sure, it was where the computer was set up, and the phone and fax, and where I did all my work for *Heights*. But it was also where I gravitated to for relaxation, for reading, for talking with ghosts and other family members.

'He's not going to come out when I'm here, is he?' Walker asked when we'd both been quiet a while.

Of course I knew whom he meant. 'Dad? No, I have a feeling he's not. It may take too much energy for a full . . . manifestation, when there's more than one person around.'

'We just need to build up a strong psychic rapport. Isn't that right, Cousin Mickey?' he called to the air. I suppose he could feel, as I did, my dad's vague presence. Too elusive to materialise that night.

I just remembered something Dan the RC priest said when he was performing my father's funeral service. 'Today's All Souls' Day?' I asked Walker.

He reflected a moment, working out the dates. 'I believe it is, yes,' he confirmed. 'Are you going to pray for Mickey's immortal soul so he'll get into heaven?'

'Not I,' I answered. 'Dad wouldn't care much for heaven, I should think. And I'm sure my prayers would only count against him.' I contemplated whether prayer or other such symbolic gestures could put my father's soul to rest so he'd no longer walk the earth as a ghost. 'Besides,' I added, 'I don't want him to move on.'

Walker merely glanced at me and nodded his understanding.

Next morning I was first up again. I had a fairly early flight to catch, while Walker didn't need to be back in Belfast until late. When I was putting on one of the new shirts I'd bought, he asked: 'Are you planning to wash the old ones?'

'I'll have them done in London,' I said. I liked my shirts nicely pressed and hated doing the job myself.

'In that case,' he said, looking up from his scrambled eggs, 'leave me the new blue shirt.'

11

LONDON AND MISS KATE

A lways, always a pleasure to return to London.

It was lovely arriving rested in Bloomsbury, my old home-from-home, after the hop across the Irish Sea instead of a debilitating trek across the broad Atlantic. And I was early enough for a relaxing, chilling sit on an old broken bench in the park outside my hotel at Tavistock Square. I was enjoying the cold air's wonderful smells of dead leaves, the tranquil statue of Mahatma Gandhi, and a snack of rhubarb custard yogurt when Paul Mason, my photographer, caught up with me.

'Ready to go?' I asked, half rising.

'Take your time,' he answered, sitting down beside me. 'I'm parked on the square.' Despite my penchant for walking or public transport, Paul preferred driving when he was on assignment, especially for hauling his equipment.

'Been busy?' I enquired between little plastic spoonfuls of the tart yogurt.

'I've had quieter periods,' he said. 'I'll tell you about it later. A bit of turmoil, that's all ... You're looking very ... something. Serene?'

His observation surprised me. Serene? Paul didn't know about my father's death. I told him the reason for my unplanned visit to Ireland and he expressed his condolences.

'Still, you seem to be coping. Usually you're a bit stressed when you come over to London. This time you're very relaxed. I thought at first ...'

'Yes?'

'I know now it's inappropriate, but I did think you might be in the thralls of a new romance.'

I didn't respond, not knowing what to say.

It was just as well that Paul drove us out to Hampstead Heath, because we'd never have found the unmarked street travelling on foot. Paul, however, kept a stash of detailed street maps in his glove box.

The actress's residence was a townhouse, part of a row. We were greeted in the first-storey foyer by a small, dark-haired woman – not an extraordinary figure, although pleasant-faced and instantly likeable.

'Mr McDermott?' she proffered with a tentative smile. 'I'm Katie Halberstadt.'

I recognised Katherine Halberstadt from the faxes sent to me. Her face was also familiar from somewhere else.

'*That Time*,' I said, perhaps too brusquely, before I caught myself. 'I'm sorry. I just remembered.'

That Time was a play about a middle-aged woman – a good fifteen or twenty years older than the woman before me now – who is thrown back to her youth to revisit a long-since-played-out romance.

'You've a good memory,' she responded in surprise. 'That was a few years back. And short-lived, at that.'

'And it was not a singing part,' I recalled. 'Very understated. I liked it very much. I should have realised it was you.'

'You're very kind,' she said, leading me and Paul into a sitting room, where Paul began to set up his equipment. '*That Time* was hardly noticed – at that time or ever.'

'The timing wasn't right, was all. The play was actually quite good.'

We spent a pleasant two hours or so talking about her musical training, her past theatrical appearances, her current West End role in *Cecilia*, about her marriage to a city barrister, and about her upcoming, second compact disc. And she agreed to my standard, offhand request that I might contact her again to fill in details for the article.

The interview went well enough, but not to my complete satisfaction. Although I enjoyed the woman's company, her modesty was somewhat self-effacing. I wondered whether I could bring across the underlying strength of her presence in an article. I doubted whether Paul would have better luck in his photography.

As we drove away, I was nagged by a fear that my article for *Heights* would only be adequate. At worst Katie Halberstadt would come across as attractive, intelligent and professional. But lacking a fire that I knew existed and couldn't evoke.

'Fancy a night out tomorrow?' I asked Paul.

He raised an eyebrow. He'd worked with me long enough by now to suspect what I had in mind. 'With all my gear? We'll need permission to shoot in the theatre.'

'In the dressing room,' I said. 'We'll get consent before we use the prints. Can you make your outfit more portable and less conspicuous?'

'I have a walking stick that's a slimline tripod. Not as versatile, but it'll do. Close-up lens only, I take it?'

'You've got the picture.' I smiled. 'Or you will tomorrow.'

A fax transmission was waiting for me at the hotel – only nine pages, due to Jack's quick intervention. Prosser had another project for me in London. The gist of the communication was that a producer had contracted the rights to make an American version of a now-ended British television comedy. *Heights* would not normally be concerned with such a likely flop, but the star signed for the American show was the old borsch-belt comedian Melvin Green, who would tailor the role unreservedly to his persona and thus ensure its success. Even *Heights* was having a hard time getting an interview with Green, so Prosser's plan was to research everything available about the British production as background to finagle a meeting with Green. I had doubts myself, feeling that the American comedian would not be impressed by our strategy.

I spent much of the next day at the British Broadcasting Corporation offices, reviewing tapes of *Both My Houses*, the British comedy soon to be Americanised. The premise was that the star, played by British actor Randy Phillips, has been made redundant and is too overeducated and overqualified for any available job. So, he trashes his curriculum vitae, takes on a Cockney accent and starts at the bottom, taking a job as an errand boy at a fashion house, where (farcically transferring his former architectural skills to designing women's fashions) he quickly rises to the top but has to keep up the Cockney pretence to maintain his rags-to-riches success. The show was very silly, filled with slapstick, incredible lapses in logic and an abundance of easy ribald jokes, but it had endured through eight seasons.

As the episodes unfolded on the monitor in front of me, my own plan took shape. I'd interview Randy Phillips and get his take on the revival of his masterpiece in America as *House by Me* (a play on 'how's by me', which fell flat, I thought), with Green in his pivotal role. At worst, *Heights* would have a retrospective of the career of the British actor, a cult favourite. With luck and chutzpah, Jack, my associate, could approach Melvin Green with my Phillips article in hand and challenge the comedian's ego. I was counting on Green jumping at the opportunity – a virtual rebuttal, a chance to highlight his own comic genius and to contrast his re-creation of the show for American tastes.

I was fortunate that Randy Phillips agreed to an interview, even after my full disclosure. The only catch was that I'd have to stay over through Tuesday, when he'd be in London for the day. I had no objection.

That evening Paul and I met at the theatre early, with photographic and writing gear concealed. Our seats were in the stalls – far enough back so we weren't likely to be seen from the stage.

I'd seen the play *Cecilia* once before and was familiar with its background (more so after reading the programme during pre-performance drinks). The story was not based on Frances Burney's eighteenth-century work but on a rather obscure three-volume nineteenth-century novel. The story is a litany of tragedies. Young, proud and opinionated, Cecilia is suddenly orphaned and has to take work as a maid. The master of the house is drawn to her strength of will and intelligence, and they have an affair. Pregnant, she is discharged by the man's wife. She is next found on the streets, impoverished and devastated by the death of the child soon after its birth. The play then jumps years ahead. Cecilia, now a housekeeper, re-encounters her former lover. But now she realises that his renewed desire is mere self-indulgence, and she coldly rejects his advances.

The role of Cecilia is quite demanding, yet enviable for a good actress. The audience must be left wondering about the depths of Cecilia's love for the man during the early infatuation and when she rejects him years later. The audience has to know that her feelings are strong but controlled by her will. It is, moreover, a singing role. As a musical, *Cecilia* tends toward monotony – challenging tunes with unmemorable and prosaic lyrics. And yet, I'll concede, one or two of the songs could be downright haunting.

When the actress playing Cecilia came on stage, I nudged Paul. 'Did you hear anything about a stand-in tonight?' I asked.

'That's her,' he said.

I had to trust his photographer's eye. I looked again. I knew a lot of make-up would be involved in creating the character of Cecilia, but the woman on stage was taller, and much thinner and plainer than the woman I'd interviewed in Hampstead the day before. Knowing it was all illusion, I still needed to study her closely through the first scenes before I really believed she was the same woman.

The voice, the entire character was ... incredible. The words she sang were simple, sometimes ludicrous in their phrasing. Still, the miserable creature was somehow irresistible in all her pathetic, straightforward despair – with a constant undercurrent of pride and determination. I was mesmerised by Katherine Halberstadt's Cecilia.

We slipped away to the stage door before curtain calls ended. I passed along my business card, with the mere exaggerated notation 'a few moments, please – time of essence' written on the back. To my relief, we were given entry and led to the Miss Halberstadt's dressing room.

'You indicated some urgency, Mr McDermott,' she said from behind a partially opened door.

'Yes. I need to speak with you before you're completely out of character. While you're taking off your make-up.'

She hesitated, looking indecisively at both me and Paul, aware that he would have his camera.

'Forgive me for reminding you. You did agree to a further meeting.' God, I thought, I'm beginning to sound as melodramatic as the play. Then again, melodrama seemed called for at that moment.

'I had no idea you might mean . . .' she protested. 'I could, in clear conscience, refuse.'

'You could,' I allowed. I may be determined, but I would not force an unwilling interview.

Silently, she opened the door and backed away. I was right that she had not immediately abandoned the character of Cecilia. She still had the posture, the demeanour. And, at the same time, the reluctance of an actor to be caught in transition.

'I don't know . . .' she hesitated.

'Please sit. Go on with what you were doing,' I said. Paul was already setting up his walking-stick tripod and taking light readings. I touched her hand gently. I wished, at that moment, that I could give some assurance that I wouldn't hurt her in any way, that I wouldn't print a word or a picture without her approval. Instead I asked, in a gentle voice, 'You do understand?'

She nodded once, acquiescing. Then she sat at the dressing table and slowly began to remove the carefully applied make-up, which was not as heavily laid on as I'd thought. The artifice relied primarily on character presentation.

'Tell me about Cecilia,' I continued.

She looked once more at Paul before obliterating his presence from her consciousness. She talked then about Cecilia – not about what Katherine Halberstadt drew from to create the character, but about who the character was and what she felt. I remarked on the 'love' song Cecilia sings when she admits her continued love to the man responsible for her past misery and when she rejects him all the same.

'It is a telling scene, isn't it?' she remarked. 'A telling title as well – "I did not choose".'

'Would you sing me a few bars?' I asked.

She was reluctant, I could tell, but she obliged me. She picked up the song lightly, as though she intended to merely run through the melody and iterate the words. Even unaccompanied, she completely re-entered the role and the emotions of Cecilia. Her voice broke and she stopped. Her voice had also broken during the song in the performance and probably did so naturally most every night, at roughly the same point. There was a light flow of tears on Katie's face, which mixed with the last remains of the character's make-up. There, I knew, as the shutter on Paul's camera clicked, would be the telling photo in the spread, the critical moment in the article, when the reader could grasp some understanding of the character's boundless passion – a passion the actress must find with every performance and must carefully wash away each night. Paul would capture the picture; I'd have to find the words. That was my challenge, the reason I worked for *Heights*.

12

TWO HOMES

In all, I was enjoying my time in London. It had been too long since I'd been there on assignment. Being back in the saddle, as it were, in the midst of London's theatre world, was refreshing. And stimulating. I really needed to be out in the field more often.

The Randy Phillips interview on Tuesday was a lark. We met at the BBC offices, then taxied out to a chilly Hyde Park for photos where I was lucky enough to catch Paul. I enjoyed talking with Phillips. The actor was a dapper little man, very stiff and very slapstick – an absurd blend of Clifton Webb and Charlie Chaplin.

'Are you planning a British sequel to *Both My Houses*?' I asked, alluding to his business that day at the BBC.

'A sequel? No, the Beeb doesn't like to revisit the scene of the crime.' He explained, 'We are discussing a totally new venture. Still in the draft stage.'

'A new comedy?' I persisted. 'Can't you give me a hint

what it's about?'

'Oh no, no, no. Absolutely not. Top secret, you know.' An impish smile escaped. 'But if you can imagine a retirement home resident saddled with an unplanned newborn daughter, you wouldn't be far off.'

I laughed. 'I'll be looking forward to it.' I didn't care any more whether we scooped an interview with Green. Phillips by himself would carry off a well-rounded article.

After we'd seen Randy Phillips off to Victoria station, Paul invited me to a home-cooked dinner, at his fiancée's home outside the city. Jeanne was a bright and fetchingly amusing woman. Her cheerful air reminded me of Marnie Dodd. And I thought of Marnie's quick smile and her bright, clear eyes.

I was home in Magilligan on Wednesday night – late, due to air traffic congestion. The house was dark and cold. For a change, there was no rain. The temperature had dropped and a brisk wind tried in vain to rattle the double-glazed windows. For the first time, I turned up the central heating.

I heated a beef stew Jane had left in the freezer. There was mail addressed to Dad – bills. It depressed me to think that I'd have to arrange for incoming bills to be paid, because bills reminded me that I'd have to decide what to do with the house. I hadn't even dealt with Dad's ashes yet; I felt guilty for every moment I kept them confined in the urn.

After dinner I phoned Marnie.

'Hi. It's Tom McDermott. I was wondering if you're still up for a boat ride this weekend. You know – what you suggested. A quasi-sightseeing, quasi-fishing expedition.'

'Yes. I thought you might be leaving before then.' She sounded surprised, in a positive way. 'Saturday would be good, if the weather holds. You'll be coming over here?' she asked.

'I should spend some time with the Jamie McDermotts. I

could stay over Saturday night, I suppose. They have been expecting me.'

'That'll work. I can get a boat in the early afternoon. Fishing's not as good then, but that's not important, is it?'

'No,' I agreed.

I wasn't feeling talkative – I'd rather wait to see Marnie in person – so I excused myself, as soon as I could, to phone Uncle Jamie and make the other half of my arrangements.

'Tommy, boy!' he greeted me. 'When will we be seeing you?' I was silenced for a heartbeat by his voice, which initially sounded much like my father's.

'I'll be driving over to Donegal Saturday morning, if that's all right,' I said. 'I'll be out for a while in the afternoon. Boating. Do you know Marnie Dodd?'

'Marnie, is it? We know the Dodds well. So it's Marnie you're going out with? Whose boat are you taking?'

'I have no idea,' I had to admit.

'No matter. I'll be talking with the young lady anyway. You'll bring her for dinner afterwards. You'll be staying Saturday night, then. Why don't you come Friday? We're always here.'

I thanked him but begged off with the valid excuse that I didn't know whether I'd be finished with my work for *Heights* by then.

'Well then, Saturday. You'll need the directions.'

'Just a minute. I'll get a pen.'

'No need, no need,' he rushed in. 'I understand you have a fax machine.' How did he know that? 'So do I,' he said proudly, 'for the B & B. I'll fax you the directions. We've even got a little map Alice sketched out!'

With that, we rang off and I was left alone with the work I suddenly didn't feel like doing. I'd finished both interviews and had already couriered back to the States the photos Paul had developed and sent on to me at the hotel, along with my handwritten summaries of what the two articles would cover. I hadn't done any work the previous evening after dinner with Paul and Jeanne. It was Guy Fawkes Night after all – when fireworks and bonfires and roasted chestnuts held priority.

Now I sat down at the computer and went through the mechanical task of transcribing the articles I'd roughly composed in longhand. After saving the second document, I sat back, looked at the screen, scrolled through the text, thought about some rewriting, found my mind wandering, and closed the document. Looking for distraction, I scooped out a wad of receipts from my luggage and began preparing an expense report. The task only took ten minutes. I went back to the articles, staring blanking at one, then the other, with no success.

'Where is my mind? Dad?' I asked aloud.

If he was there, he didn't answer.

I decided to go out, to work off the restlessness. For the first time, I put on gloves and bundled my coat. I headed out to the road on foot, taking special care in the absence of footpaths. In the pub it was a sports night and much too noisy. I ordered a pint of beer, finished it quickly, then returned to the chilled night air. I knew it was not as cold as I felt. It couldn't possibly be cold enough to snow; the dew on the grass hadn't even frosted.

In my absence, I was grateful to discover, the house had warmed up throughout and was once again cosy.

'Tom,' I heard a voice call from the study. I took time to hang my coat before I went in.

'Dad,' I greeted him as I entered the room. I poured two glasses of the *poitín* left behind by Walker.

'Home brew,' my ghostly father commented. 'Excellent.'

I tossed him a copper-alloy penny from my pocket.

'What's this?' he asked.

'Penny for the Guy!' I said.

He laughed. 'You've already seen to another of the Guy

Fawkes customs, you know. The bonfire. You know what a bonfire is, don't you? A fire for burning bones. In short, a cremation.'

'A "bone" fire. Interesting,' I acknowledged. Frankly, the synchronicity – the overlap of the holiday customs and the contact with my deceased father's spirit – was beginning to overwhelm me. To be accurate, it was not so much the bizarre events as my own complacency about them that had me concerned. My life had been shaken up dramatically, and eventually I'd have to integrate all the changes.

'Why are you here?' I asked with uncharacteristic impatience. 'Why do I see you?'

He shrugged. 'If I'm going to haunt any place, why not here? And why shouldn't you see me? You've got the skill.'

'From Great-great-granddad Ruairí Finney, right? And he really was one of the little people?'

'Little people? Of course not. Ruairí was rather tall.'

'Sorry. Slip of the tongue. Gentle people, I should have said.'

'He was supposed to be descended from one of the *Daoine sídhe*, but you'd have to ask him about that yourself.'

I was exasperated. 'Dad! Ruairí Finney has been dead for a hundred years!'

'So what? I've been dead for a couple of weeks now and you're talking to me.'

He had me there. 'Why is that exactly? Why am I talking to you? I've never seen ghosts before.'

'You had to start sometime.'

I ignored his daft philosophy. 'And why are you the only dead person I see? Why not Grandma? She died in this house, didn't she?'

I couldn't rile his spirit. 'I imagine Mum and Da will be around by and by. They always liked the December holidays. And Eamon. He was particularly fond of Boxing Day.'

'Dad!'

'Ben, now. I think his spirit's long since moved on. One can't say absolutely.'

'Dad,' I repeated more calmly.

He motioned me to sit. I lowered myself onto the rocking chair's footrest.

'Tom. My Tom. It's not ghosts that have you in a mood.'

I gestured noncommittally.

He continued: 'Why aren't you finishing your work right now? Why haven't you dumped my ashes already? Not to put too fine a point on it, why are *you* here?'

I couldn't answer. I wasn't on vacation. I'd arranged for and stayed through the funeral – five days ago. I could 'dump' Dad's ashes anywhere, any time, for all he cared about them. My interviews were over, although I'd been quite glad to have them and had welcomed the excuse to extend my stay. Even so, I didn't need to work on the articles here. Normally I'd be on the next plane back to New York, to finish the assignments, get them behind me and move on.

Why procrastinate? Why linger? It wasn't like me. I didn't have an answer for him or myself.

I wished my father would sing something or even ask me to – any diversion would do. But he didn't say anything else. He sipped his drink and sat back in the upholstered chair. I got up from the footrest, lowered myself into the rocking chair, propped my feet, tasted my drink and opened my mind as best I could.

'Why am I still here?' I muttered to myself.

Somnus brevis II

TOM AND MARNIE IN THE PAST

When I finally crept into the solitary bed in my bedroom in my own inherited house, I dreamt about the few visitors to the house since my arrival.

'Goodnight, Walker,' I said, as I again left the guest room in the dream.

''Night, son,' he answered. I glanced back to see that Walker had metamorphosed into my dad.

Instead of going to bed myself, I stepped outside through a door opening from the front parlour into a backyard where the study extension did not yet exist. It was twilight. A bite to the air — jacket weather. My father was standing with hunched shoulders and upturned collar against the chill, watching the Donegal sunset. He was several years younger than I.

'Evening,' he greeted me, as though I were a neighbour passing by on the road.

'Evening.'

He drew on a newly lit cigarette.

'That'll kill you, you know.'

He looked at the burning end of the cigarette. 'This? It's no worse a habit than drinking. Safer, if you're driving.'

'Cancer,' I countered.

He shrugged. The reddened western sky was slowly darkening.

'Hear you're going to America,' I prompted.

'Next week. I'll be in Scranton, Pennsylvania. Some friends have arranged a job for me in a restaurant.'

'Isn't work in an Irish–American restaurant a bit of a cliché?'

'Is it?' he asked innocently. 'If it is, it's less so than becoming a copper. Or a priest.'

'True,' I agreed.

The sky was much darker now. I could barely see my future dad's young face, which was illuminated from time to time by his still-burning cigarette.

'I'm waiting for Jamie,' he explained. 'He has a few quid to spare this week. He's just gone to pick up his girl,' he said, nodding towards the land across the lough. 'Alice.'

'By boat?' I asked.

'Nae. Too cold for that. He's borrowed a car, hasn't he? Alice will stay over here with her aunt and uncle.'

All the red had disappeared from the western sky, and the only lights came from the sparsely scattered houses and the headlights of infrequent passing cars. One such rare car turned into the side road and drove up to the house. I could barely see the face of the female passenger. A young, slimmer Jamie McDermott leaned out the driver's window and shouted to his brother Michael. 'Let's go!'

Dad turned to me. 'You coming?' he asked.

'Not tonight,' I said. 'Another time. Thanks.'

With that, young Mickey McDermott got into the back seat of the car and sped off with his brother and his brother's future wife to join their friends. I went back inside.

When I reached the large bedroom at the end of the hall, it was mid-morning. I was undressed, apparently just getting out of bed. I peeked through the curtains into a brightly sunlit yard.

'What is it?' the woman's voice asked from beneath the bed covers. She was, of course, Marnie.

'Only the boys,' I said. 'Having a catch.'

Outside the boys were playing with a ball – my dad and his brothers, all five of them, the same ages as in the photograph hanging on the bedroom wall. They undoubtedly had no idea that one of them would soon die of illness, that there would be a Second World War that would take the second-born son, that the youngest would take up life on the other side of the lough with a woman he'd not yet met, and that the next youngest brother, my dad, would live half his life in America before returning to this home.

I heard a stirring from the covers. 'Come back to bed.'

13

THE NORTHERN COAST

The next was a busy work day. Fortified by a high-carbohydrate breakfast and strong coffee – as well as the previous night's dream – I was able to channel my energies again. By late afternoon I'd finished both reviewing the new material that'd been faxed over to me the night before and editing the Randy Phillips article, and had sent them speeding through phone lines to America. Later in the evening Jack would call to tell me that he'd used the Phillips article as leverage to get an interview with Melvin Green.

In the meantime, the Halberstadt piece required much greater attention. I was restless again – waiting on a creative breakthrough, squinting for it, pacing for it, trying to evoke it by drumming my fingers on the desk, until finally my attention failed and I found myself gazing in distraction out the windows, letting my mind drift somewhere out into the ether. As soon as I turned my back on the problem the answer came to me. What I'd been looking for was a way to present the moment of transition when Katie was both herself and the character she was portraying. The solution was to tie a quotation from Katie to a line from her character.

The concept was simple, but execution required a major rewrite to highlight the subtle perceptions brought out in Katie's performance and reflected in Paul's photographs. I worked late into the night, reread the article during breakfast, then sent it off with only minor changes.

In spite of my struggles, I had finished ahead of schedule, but decided to treat Friday as a free day, a holiday, instead of moving up my visit to Donegal. I picked up a couple of disposable cameras, then set out for a leisure drive along the northern coast. It felt terribly good to travel loose, to stretch my wings.

I drove first to Downhill to shoot the row of houses at the base of the cliffs, the rail tunnel driven through the hillside, and the rain-weighted sandy beach. Atop the hill sat the empty shell of Downhill House, built by the so-called Earl Bishop, the same Bishop of Derry who'd donated the property for St Aidan's church in Duncrun. All that remained of the manor house were sad, naked walls exposed to the elements.

My stops were brief, to capture scenes key to my frame of mind. In Articlave, the charming village's solid stone buildings. In Coleraine, a bridge across the River Bann and the old town centre. In Portstewart, the harbour crescent of shops. Moving into County Antrim, I passed the Dunluce Castle ruins and the Bushmills Distillery, but decided to save them for a future visit. This trip, I was keen to see the Giant's Causeway.

The causeway is composed of thousands of massive hexagonal basalt columns tightly packed together – resembling stacks of unsharpened pencils – whose construction is attributed to Finn McCool, the Ulster giant of legend, who built the path to reach either (according to differing legends) his foe or his giantess girlfriend in Staffa, an island in the Scottish Hebrides. The gale-force winds (remnants of a hurricane come over from America) added a rough elemental touch suitable to a giant's passage.

When I was thoroughly mist-drenched and bone-chilled, and enjoying the wet cold, I took the bus back up to the car park. The car heater's blast dried my wet jacket and warmed my bones, while a play on Radio Ulster kept me entertained on the drive home.

Home. Hot bath. Tea. Bit of a nap. Then over to the Robert McDermotts' house to talk them into joining me at the pub, as it was Friday night. It was an agreeable way to round out an enjoyable, leisure day.

They must have been intrigued by what an outsider would find interesting to see and do around their home turf, because they wanted to hear all the details of my day. I think also that, because they were always together with family if they weren't at work, they were curious about what a single person does on his own.

'I just putter about,' I said.

'Don't you get lonely? Or bored?' Jane asked.

'Bored? Never. I only get bored when I'm with people I don't like. I'm never bored on my own, because I'm always free to do something that I'd want to do. I'm more likely to run out of time than things to do.'

'That would be like Mickey,' Uncle Robert said. 'Even as a wee boy, he'd spend hours amusing himself, not needing the company of a single living being.' Yes, that sounded like Dad. I realised we had that trait in common.

Robbie added: 'We were worried he might be lonely when he came back. But he said sometimes he prefers to be alone.'

That too sounded like me. But I used to wonder whether

Dad must not sometimes feel deeply lonely.

'What did you do today then?' Jane asked.

I told them about my drive in the rain, and about clambering over the Giant's Causeway to try to get some good shots with my cheap camera. And I told them about my rambling through the empty hull of Downhill House and my wondering how it had come to that condition.

'I drive by Downhill twice a day, and I never even think about it,' Robbie told me. 'It's been like that as long as I can remember.'

But Uncle Robert's memory was more extensive. 'It's not so long since it was occupied,' he said. 'I remember the RAF using the house in the Second World War.'

'Was it bombed?' I asked.

'No. It just fell into disuse after the war. Eventually the furnishings were taken away and the interior was stripped. Nobody had a use for it any more.'

Sad, the changes time could bring. I learned that even sparsely peopled Magilligan once housed hundreds of families in its small townlands. But that was before the mid-nineteenth-century's famine years, and the area never came close to regaining its earlier populations.

It was easy to talk that night because it was unusually quiet in the pub. No crowds for a Friday night. Unquestionably off season. And there was no sport on television. Even more unusual was the presence of a musician at this particular pub. The manager's daughter or niece was picking out tunes on an acoustic guitar by the burning hearth. She'd said hello when we entered the half-empty place and later came over to our table.

'I hear you can sing,' she said. I sighed to myself. I should get used to everyone knowing who I was. I tried to demur from her request that I sing, but was overruled by my companions. The girl pulled up a chair and accompanied my humble rendition of 'Good Night, Irene' – more

Leadbelly version than Weavers.

Even though I successfully begged off an encore, our table was treated to a free round of drinks. Not bad, I thought. If I ever gave up my regular job, I could surely become accustomed to singing for my supper. Or at least for a bevvy.

14

ASHES TO OCEAN

Next morning I packed the essentials for my visit across the lough – a light suitcase with a few clothes and the psychically weighty urn filled with my father's cremated remains. A new take on packing up my troubles in an old kitbag, eh?

The way to Uncle Jamie's took me down towards Derry, but then across the River Foyle and up its western side to the opposite shores of Lough Foyle, into the Inishowen peninsula. I almost missed the border-crossing from Northern Ireland's County Derry into the Republic's County Donegal, because there were no guards, no border check during the cease-fire. Only the change in road signs – from miles to kilometres, and from English-only to bilingual names – indicated that I had technically crossed into another country.

Whether figured in kilometres or miles, the drive was forty-five minutes from my home to Moville, a hillside village with a striking and reassuring view – surely not so much as three miles across the water – of Magilligan's low, grassy dunes backed by the dark brooding mass of Binevenagh.

I had no difficulty finding my uncle's bed-and-breakfast from the directions Jamie had faxed me. But I barely had time to say hello to my kin before Marnie appeared and whisked me off to beat the rain showers and choppy waters forecast for later in the afternoon.

The Greencastle harbour had been expanded over the years to accommodate commercial fishing vessels, one of which was taking on chipped ice by a conveyor as we arrived. In a small part of the harbour, on the inland side of the commercial pier, dozens of smaller boats, in various states of repair, were huddled together like . . . well, like sardines, I suppose. I was expecting we'd be taking out something along the lines of one of the simple recreational motor boats I saw. What we boarded was a small fishing boat with a cabin above deck.

'Trevor's,' Marnie explained. 'They only took the one boat out today.'

'I see', was all I had time to say, because we were suddenly too busy casting off for me to ask who Trevor was. Marnie handled the boat with competence and familiarity. We were soon out of the crowded, sheltered harbour of shoulder-to-shoulder boats and into the lough and the wide-open Atlantic Ocean. We briskly passed Magilligan Point. Of course, I couldn't see my house, but I managed to snap a few quick photos of the dunes obscuring my house's flat, low neighbourhood – the Irish netherlands.

We dropped anchor well within sight of the Irish coastline. To the north I glimpsed the vague outline of what could have been a Scottish island, though it could have been an illusion created by cloud striations. I knew that the Faeroes lay at a distance beyond the Hebrides, then eventually Iceland and the Arctic Ocean. Here, though, the climate was far from arctic – with sea and air warmed by the Gulf Stream from the Americas.

For appearance's sake, we fastened hookless fishing poles into brackets welded onto the boat. Shielded from any curious shore-based eyes by the bulk of the craft, I took the urn from my suitcase and removed the tape covering the broken seal. I waited until the breezes died, then, while Marnie watched in silence, I unceremoniously emptied the contents into the ocean and let the waves rinse the urn and its top clean. Some of the ash and the larger, heavier remains sank immediately, while other flakes lingered, suspended in the salt water.

'Very neatly done,' Marnie commented.

'Thank you.'

'We should stay here a while, I suppose.'

'I suppose.' The awkwardness of our enterprise was dissipating.

I walked about the deck until I found a perspective of the land suitable for photography and contemplation. The coastlines of Counties Antrim, Derry and Donegal stretched to the horizons under a clouded autumnal sun. I stood absorbed in thought for some time.

'Do you know what you're looking at?' Marnie asked when she thought I'd been given enough time alone.

'The house is hidden by the dunes,' I replied. 'It should be' – I pointed – 'just there.'

'I believe you're right. I recognise one of the taller houses near yours.'

We were silent a while before I spoke again. I was looking at Magilligan overall, lounging in the mist.

'It's an awfully lonely, uninviting place. Look at it. It's like a big, flat delta opening into the frigid North Atlantic. It has an empty look. I know it was once densely populated – a hundred, hundred-fifty years ago. There's no local economy now to speak of. The fishing trade's gone. No linen industry. Well yes, farming still, and grazing. But otherwise nothing to attract people. Except a rather nice beach.'

'Presently spotted with mysterious black ashes coming from the vicinity of the boat.'

'True.'

'And intermittently barricaded for the British Army's rifle ranges.'

'Also true,' I conceded.

'And?'

I sighed. 'And there's a lot of green – grasses and all – but hardly any trees in the valley. It's very wet – all the time, by what I've seen. I don't know if the ocean ever gets wild enough to flood the area, but if it does, it certainly would.'

'Stands to reason.'

I sighed again. 'At the end of the day, it's desolate. Very desolate.'

Marnie had put her arm on mine, then taken my hand in hers. Or had I made that advance?

'So why do you like it?' she asked. 'Will you be sad leaving it?'

'Miserable. I don't know why. In some ways it's like Hull – where my apartment is, in New York. Hull has some prosperous neighbourhoods, yet the town overall is very depressing. And depressed. Nothing has replaced the business establishments that've closed down over the past twenty-some years. The downtown area has a great broad street flanked on both sides by empty shops. I like the solitude but there's nothing to keep me there. No roots. After three years I don't even know my neighbours in the same building. Here,' I concluded, 'there's too much of the opposite. Everyone seems to know who I am and what I'm doing.'

'It's only your family that cares one way or another. For

the most part.'

'I suppose,' I agreed, tired now of hearing about myself. 'You know, Ms Dodd, you're one of those people who know everything about me, while I know practically nothing about you.'

'You know plenty. My name. Where I live, more or less – not far from your uncle's. You'll see. You know I teach English.'

'Why English?'

'I like it, that's why. And I'm fairly good at teaching it, I like to think.'

'I'm sure you are. What about your family? Are your parents alive? Do you have any sisters or brothers?'

'A brother, married. My parents live farther inland. You might meet them another time.' I might like that.

'You play the violin,' I continued, 'quite beautifully.'

'So you said once before. Too much flattery, Mr McDermott.' She took her arm away from mine; any longer contact might signify more than we could handle, God forbid. I didn't think either of us was prepared for any serious developments. She walked a few steps away; I had to turn to face her when she spoke again.

'How was London? You didn't mention your trip.' She was now sitting on a platform and leaned back against the sloping outside wall of the pilot house. I sat beside her, stretching my legs and enjoying the meagre sunshine.

'London was . . . excellent. London is always good for me. I could stay there . . . I'd like to spend a lot more time there.' I would, really. 'Do you get over there much?'

'From time to time. I have a girlfriend I stay with.'

'That's good.' A pause, as we watched the clouds – dull grey sheets, no fluffy white animal shapes.

'Did you see any shows?' Marnie asked.

'Just the one – *Cecilia*. To fill out my interview with one of the performers. Have you seen it?'

'No.'

All this time we were sitting, reclining side by side. Relaxing, not bothering to face each other.

'It's a rather strange piece. Hard to describe. I can send you my article when it's printed; that'll give you some idea.'

'I'd like that. Thank you.'

'It will have pictures,' I added inanely.

'I've been to New York,' she said lightly, changing the tone. 'I stayed in Yonkers with some friends.'

'Really? I had the impression you didn't like to travel,' I admitted.

'Not often,' she admitted in return. 'And not for terribly long. Every now and then I do enjoy a bit of travel outside the country.'

'As long as you can get back before you get homesick.'

'You've been talking with Walker, I gather. He used to try talking me into moving to Belfast. But I never had an aching to go.'

'You two were . . . You were a couple?'

'We've gone out a time or two,' she conceded. 'I've known him since we were pups.'

'Pups?'

'Um-hm,' she murmured. She had lost interest in the topic.

And then we were drifting. Not the boat – Marnie and I. Lying ever so close. Not touching, yet keenly aware of each other's presence. Not a thought, no expectations, no need to speak. We lay like that for an eternity, warmed by the dim sun and sheltered from the breezes blowing across the boat's railings above our heads.

Marnie was the first to break the reverie. I saw her standing above me, looking down into my face.

'We can move on now. It'll be obvious that we've given up on the fishing. We'll have a little pleasure cruise – going miles and miles away from home, we're so brave,' she kidded me.

We cruised west to areas I hadn't seen – past Malin Head, catching a glimpse behind Fanad Head of Ballymastocker Bay, where the Knockalla Mountains run down to the mouth of Lough Swilly, beyond Horn Head, and circling widely around Tory Island to view a perspective of Donegal's irregular west coast before our return to Inishowen Head and into the calmer waters of Lough Foyle. I enjoyed Marnie's company, whether we were talking or not. She let me take her picture when we returned to port, with no dissemblance about her appearance and no attempt to ruin a casual shot with a self-conscious pose.

Back on land, I drove Marnie home to her flat in a two-storey house, a mere street away from Uncle Jamie's. I had to decline her offer of a skeeg of tea – Jamie's family would be expecting me by now – so we didn't move far from the threshold of her door.

'The other night,' Marnie began. 'You and Walker really were talking about ghosts, weren't you?'

'Yes.' I thought we'd come around to that subject at some point.

'You have seen your father's ghost then?'

'Yes.'

'I don't know whether I'd want that … ability. To see ghosts. Sometimes I've felt something, like a presence when no one was there. And I've heard noises in old houses – creaks and possibly footsteps. Who hasn't? But if I ever actually saw a ghost … I couldn't be sceptical after that.'

I wasn't sure I got her point. 'It's important for you to be sceptical?'

She smiled. 'I like to keep all options open.'

'I see.' I didn't see at all.

'I'll see you later at dinner then?' I said.

She hesitated then shook her head. 'There are a few things I have to do,' she responded vaguely, as a lame explanation. 'Anyway, you should spend time with your family.'

My disappointment must have shown. She smiled placatingly. 'Wait here a moment. I have something for you.'

I waited outside by the car. In less than two minutes she returned, bearing her gift for me – a large, glossy photograph of my cousin Walker McDermott, with his professional résumé on the back. I thanked her, but I was still disappointed.

'I figure he must have left before you got a camera,' she explained.

'And you just happened to have a spare headshot.'

'A few copies he left behind.'

Left behind? At her flat? Did they have some sort of relationship after all? I wished I had some standing to be able to ask. If I were in a position to ask, I'd be in a position to be jealous. I was not.

'Will I see you again before I go?' I asked.

Her smile disappeared. 'Back to America? It's not impossible.'

During my time with her, I hadn't given any thought to returning to the States. 'I meant, before I go back to Magilligan.'

She shrugged and smiled again. Then she kissed me quickly on the cheek and walked unhurriedly back to the house. 'Goodbye,' she called over her half-turned shoulder, avoiding eye contact.

When she was inside, behind a firmly closed door, I drove the short jaunt to Uncle Jamie's. As I was bringing in my suitcase, I allowed myself a quick glance back towards Marnie's house.

The empty urn remained, carefully wrapped in a towel, in the boot of the car. Well, there was one problem resolved.

15

FAMILY ON THE OTHER SIDE

Try as I might, I couldn't understand Marnie's sudden decision to exile herself from my family's company, from my company. As she'd already phoned her regrets to Aunt Alice, there were only the three of us for the evening repast – my aunt and uncle and I. My cousin Ellen, the daughter still living at home, was down at university for some evening programme. The other cousins – Harry, Dennis and Eveline – were home with their own families.

After our warmly filling dinner of chicken, green beans and potatoes (both boiled and baked – 'go figure!' I thought, not comprehending the need for two potato dishes but enjoying both), Uncle Jamie showed me an old album from his boyhood days. There were photos of Dad I'd never seen; they helped fill out my image of him in his youth. Jamie pointed out other McDermott and Finney kin and kith, including the lively and ever-pretty Alice as a young girl. Interspersed with later photos of Jamie's own family were pictures from my parents' wedding, even of myself as a child. I'd never realised how close the brothers' contact had remained.

When evening had worn long, we went out to a pub up in Greencastle, at the edge of the rocky coast, near the harbour, although by then it was too late to discern more than a vague impression of the Derry shores across the lough.

'I wonder sometimes whether we drink too much, as a country,' Jamie commented when we settled at a table with our pints. 'There's not much else to do at night. Except watch television or read.'

'Are you an avid reader?' I asked, remembering the filled bookshelves in his home.

He nodded. 'I read like a fish.'

I had no idea what he meant, but the analogy made me laugh.

We were soon joined at the pub by Trevor the boat-loaner, who turned out (as I'd come to suspect) to be Trevor Finney, one of the cousins I'd met in Magilligan – a second cousin, I surmised – and his wife Maureen, along with Trevor's unmarried brother Declan. They were a hearty, weather-skinned trio. In age, my best guess would be somewhere between my generation and the next – late forties? early fifties?

I thanked Trevor for the use of his boat. 'What do I owe you?' I asked, reaching for my wallet.

'Put that away now,' he commanded. 'I was glad to help. The boat wasn't going to be used anyway.'

'But the fuel, at least,' I protested.

He was firm and quietly insistent. 'I know your mission. I wouldn't insult your da by accepting a penny. Letting you use the boat was the least we could do. I would have taken you out myself, if Marnie hadn't offered.'

'Well then, thank you again. I take it you didn't object to the . . . mission.'

He shook his head. 'Not for me to say. Still, I see no harm in it.'

'Nor do I,' said Uncle Jamie. Of course, I'd told him what I'd be up to on the boat. 'Nor would Michael have any objection. Ashes to ashes. Back to the elements.'

Jamie offered a toast to Dad's memory. Then we moved on to other talk, which for quite a while was mostly about fishing – Trevor's family's profession and formerly Jamie's – and consequently about the weather.

I wished Marnie were there. What business did she have tonight? School work? Couldn't that have waited? Was she tired of me already – or simply uninterested? Perhaps she didn't have a fix on her own feelings – because of an understanding she had with someone else – and needed to distance herself from me for a while?

It might even be true, as Marnie had suggested, that she thought I should spend more time with my family – particularly if she knew how many would be congregating at the pub. Besides Jamie and Alice McDermott, their son Dennis and his wife Mary, their son Harry had also showed up with his family. Word of mouth or the family grapevine also brought a number of the Finneys together that night. In addition to Trevor, Maureen and Declan, I met the boys' aunt and uncle, Kenneth and Hester Finney Gaines, who'd also brought photos of their daughter and grandchildren.

I was introduced to another branch of Finneys – Nathan Lowell, a great-uncle by marriage. His daughter and son-in-law, Cassandra and Hal, were home down in Strabane, but the next generation was represented by Cassandra Finney Willoughby, the granddaughter. Cassandra was an architect with an office cottage at the tiny harbour in Moville, where she lived with her fiancé Alec. Her brother, Robert Lowell Willoughby, had driven over from Letterkenny to meet us. In still another branch, second cousin Julian Finney, an artist, was joined by his sister and brother-in-law, Connie and Sam

Cuddihy. Members of the Finney clan were generally of fairer colouring than the McDermotts, predominantly medium and light brunettes, blondes and a few redheads.

I was dumbstruck for a moment when introduced to my cousin Kieran Finney, who, as my third cousin, was the only member present from the lineage of another son of my great-great-grandfather Ruairí Finney, descendant of the reputed interloper from the world of the gentry. Kieran was in fact the only son of the only son of the only son of Neil, the twin brother of my great-grandfather Noel Finney. He bore no resemblance to any of the McDermott brood, and indeed there was no reason why he should. Twenty- or thirty-some-year-old, crisply blue-eyed, curly auburn-haired Kieran was the living physical embodiment of the mysterious Seán Sylvanus Finney in my recent dream. Looking at him, I saw again the image of an old cottage set into a hillside and a rowboat waiting in the gentle lapping waters of a calm, isolated bay.

'Are you a fisherman by any chance?' I asked.

'Not primarily,' he answered, 'but I have an adequate grasp of the art of fishing.' He smiled – knowingly?

As it turned out, Kieran was a writer of unpublished (because unsubmitted) poetry and moderately successful, semi-bizarre contemporary gothic novels. I apologised for not knowing his work and asked about the publisher of his novels. It was a smaller house, with wide recognition but limited distribution.

'I'll send you one or two books, if you like,' he offered. 'For the novelty. I wouldn't expect you to read them. My writing's an acquired taste, you might say.'

'It could be that you need better press,' I countered. Writers' popularity often depended on the effectiveness of their publishers' support.

But Kieran didn't agree. 'No, my work really does have a limited following. A cult following, you might say. That is what I prefer. I don't want to be on anyone's best-seller list. I don't want to be a book-club selection. I feel most comfortable with a small but loyal readership who like my books well enough to keep buying them.'

'You said gothic?' I encouraged him to elaborate.

'Gothic. Mystical. Whatever. But I try not to be too obscure.' He ran a claddagh-befingered hand through his hair as he explained. 'You could call the stories psychic adventures.'

'Hmm. You've stirred my curiosity now. I'll look forward to reading them.' I wondered whether I might find myself reading stories that mirrored my own metaphysical journey since coming to this island. Or that recorded my dream about an auburn-haired ancestor from the gentry.

He looked at my face, scrutinising my character, weighing the sincerity of my interest. 'Perhaps they'll be to your liking after all.'

After Kieran had moved on, Jamie casually mentioned that he was said to bear a strong resemblance to Ruairí Finney, who in turn was supposed to be 'the dead spit' of his grandfather Seán. My head was spinning with the complex genealogy and coincidences. Kieran, like me, must be a real-life descendant of the Seán Sylvanus Finney in my dream. Could he be the actual reincarnation of Seán?

Curious, I thought. And quite curious also that, in the same generation, there should be three of us psychically linked – Walker, Kieran and I. Do the connections never end? I felt that, if I'd asked Kieran where Walker was at that moment, an image of Walker's Belfast flat or theatre or whatever would suddenly take form in the ether. Perhaps I had such a potential ability myself. If it wasn't just the beer stirring my imagination, then there surely was some genetic bond we shared – three men of about the same age, each an only child, with a common ancestor who was other than *homo sapiens*. What would be the scientific name for a member of the gentry race? *Homo gentilis?*

In all, it was a most curious night, with no singing and even more conversation than the night of Dad's funeral. And I was right in the midst of it, no longer isolated as 'the American'. I was getting to know these people, and they me.

In the course of the evening, when I'd taken a break from my conversation with Cassie Willoughby to make my way to the bar for refills, Uncle Jamie and Aunt Alice took their leave, assuring me it was all right to roll in at any hour. When I returned to Cassie, who'd been telling me about a house she had designed for a client on the western shores of Inishowen, she and her brother, Robert, were discussing how to handle some legal problem that had arisen in the construction. We compared our limited knowledge of American and Irish property law – limited knowledge, lengthy analysis.

As the evening finally came to an end, I was promised a ride from Trevor. While waiting for the group to assemble in the car park, I stood alone in the yard looking out at the black waters of the lough and the shadow of Magilligan beyond. Despite November's chill, I felt warm in the blanket of a smoky, now familiar fog.

'Perambulating melancholy, is it?' The voice was Kieran's. I turned to face him.

'Something like that,' I answered.

He nodded. Then he turned toward the dark night and called out. 'Brimsy!'

Out of nowhere a dog wandered into our company – scarcely over a foot tall, resembling a miniature collie, bluish-grey in colour. She sauntered up to Kieran, wagging her tail, waiting for his stroke on her head.

'This is Brimstone,' he said to me. 'She's a shelty.' Ah, a Shetland sheepdog.

He held her muzzle in his hands. 'Brims,' he told her, 'this is Tom. Say hello.'

She turned to me for a quick sniff and looked up into my face. She had the most fantastic pale blue eyes I've ever seen! I must have met her approval because her tail was still wagging as she waited for my attention. I bent down, letting her put her front paws on my knee while I ruffled her furry face. She rewarded me with a kiss on the nose.

'Time to go home, Brims,' Kieran called, and they slowly, literally vanished into the black night.

16

FARM LIFE

Not a clue where I was when I awoke the next morning. I was not in the room where I'd left my luggage in Uncle Jamie's B & B, I knew that. I got out of the strange, comfortable bed and looked around the dimly lit room. The house was old. I could tell by the smell. When I pushed aside the drapes and looked out the window, I didn't see the clustered buildings of Moville's centre or the coast of Lough Foyle. Hilly farmland met my gaze. Ah, yes. For all the drinking the night before, my head cleared quickly. I remembered. Rather than disturb Uncles Jamie's family with my late return to their house, Trevor had brought me back to his home, some miles away and inland from Moville. He said he'd phone Jamie about my whereabouts in the morning.

I dressed in yesterday's clothes and stumbled my way into the kitchen. There I was greeted by an older woman just entering through the back door, carrying a basket of eggs.

'Thomas,' she said in nodding. 'Good morning.'

'Morning. You must be Trevor and Declan's mum.'

'That's right. Vinnie. Short for Lavinia. Vinnie Finney, if you can credit that.' An amusing nursery-rhyme name for a non-comical woman. She was a no-nonsense hard worker, no question. Yet she had a gentle nature and seemed easy to bring to a smile.

I asked: 'Is everyone else out? I must have slept in late.'

'No matter. They're all out for the day now.' She put the eggs on a table and took out a frying pan. 'Would you like bacon? Or we've got fish – cold, if you like, or I could heat something up. You could have both.'

'Thank you, no. I'm a light eater for breakfast. The eggs would be lovely, if you have them to spare. And just some toast or plain bread.'

'Plenty of eggs. The lights in the henhouse are on a timer. It keeps the laying day longer in winter. Would you like coffee with your egg-nog?'

Egg-nog? I gathered that was a way of preparing eggs rather than the alcoholic Christmas drink I knew. 'Tea's fine if that's easier.'

'Tea's no problem. I make it strong, but there's plenty of milk to thin it out. I may have a lemon to spare.'

'I prefer it strong. No milk or lemon.'

She looked at me askew. 'You've just exploded half the stereotypes I had about Americans, you know.'

'Sorry.'

She smiled and we instantly warmed to each other. The scheme of the day was simple: since Vinnie didn't have a car, it was planned that I should call Jamie whenever I was ready to go back to Moville. Meanwhile Vinnie would get on with her chores.

'Can I help with your work?' I offered when my energising breakfast was finished. The egg-nog, I'd been pleased to learn, was a dish of eggs scrambled and fried in bacon grease.

She hesitated. 'Not much to do, this being the off season. The usual farm work, you know.'

'I'm sure I can help with something.'

Vinnie gave me a sceptical once-over, then shrugged. I suppose she concluded I might not be entirely useless.

From somewhere in the house she found me a spare pair of wellies and an old coat warmer than my own tweed jacket. It was too early in the season for snow, but the air was crisp and frosty that morning and the mud underfoot had a slightly crunchy, frozen texture. The yard was hilly and larger than I'd expected for a home farm.

'You ever milk a cow?' Vinnie asked when we reached the dairy barn.

'Once or twice,' I answered, looking over the compact herd of four variously coloured but mostly brown Jerseys. I filled the troughs where they fed while being milked, and Vinnie led the cows into place.

'You're not still milking her, are you?' I asked, nodding towards the one large cow that was obviously in the late stages of pregnancy.

Again I was the recipient of Vinnie's askance look. 'No, she's dried off. Due in a couple of months. The others are hefted ... You've got a good eye for the bovine beasties.'

'My experience isn't all that extensive,' I confessed. 'Not much beyond what I once learned to interview a cow breeder. And to get to know some of his herds.'

'You always get that involved when you write something?'

I suppose I do. 'I have to bring some background knowledge to an interview,' I explained. 'And I always like to learn more.'

Vinnie seemed satisfied with my answer. She gave me a stool and a bucket. I warmed my hands, and set to the steady task of milking. The cows munched happily on their hay and cereal. They were docile and seemed to enjoy my humming while I worked. As she mucked out the stalls, Vinnie watched silently but with a keen eye on me.

Well, I thought to myself, Marnie may be able to pilot a fishing boat, but could she milk a cow? All right, she probably could. But could she do it with my finesse? Would she be amused if she could eavesdrop on my thoughts?

When the milking was finished and the cows were back in their stalls, Vinnie and I went out to the yard to fill watering bowls and feeding racks for the sheep – black-faced Suffolks. I noticed that both ewes and rams were freely intermingling. 'Is it mating season?' I asked.

'They have to mate now so we'll have lambs in the spring.'

'Ah. I see.'

She smiled slyly. 'Don't know as much about sheep as cows, do you?'

'No,' I laughed. 'I suppose I haven't interviewed enough shepherds.'

By the time I helped Vinnie set out some mineral licks for the sheep and lugged bales of hay and sacks of feed where I was instructed, I was beginning to break a sweat. No matter. By then everything I could do to help in the yard was done.

'Why don't you head back to the house?' Vinnie suggested. 'You'll be probably wanting a proper wash-up. I'll be along in a bit. I want to take the time you saved me to check the fence for any breaks while the weather's still good.'

Marnie was waiting at the Finneys' house when I returned. I was glad to see her again. Hell, I was elated. Not that I'd give away my feelings.

'I've come for the eggs,' she said.

'Vinnie's the only one home,' I responded obliquely, as I removed the borrowed wellies and coat. 'And she's out walking the fence. Or is this a help-yourself business?'

'I can wait.'

'Did you happen to stop by Jamie's house this morning?' I asked, cockily hoping she'd been looking for me.

She smiled. 'Yes. Alice mentioned Trevor had phoned to say you'd spent the night here.'

That was what I wanted to hear. Marnie had been checking up on me.

'I missed you last night,' I admitted in return.

'Good,' she answered. 'Not that I planned for you to miss me. I really did have some work to catch up on for my classes; I can't let the students get ahead of me.' She hesitated. 'And I thought perhaps you'd seen too much of me in too short a time.'

'I won't apologise for . . . for growing fond too quickly. Scary as the prospects are.'

'I know,' she said, amused by my words.

'I did miss you,' I repeated.

'Good,' she said again. She moved in close to kiss me. I backed away – just slightly.

'I was about to take a shower,' I apologised. 'I haven't . . .'

She interrupted: 'I could . . .' Her face flushed with embarrassment at her uncharacteristic boldness. 'I'd like to be with you. I don't mean . . . I mean I'd like to be with you. That's all.'

I didn't think I was quite ready for a turbid sexual encounter just then either. Intimacy, however, would be quite pleasant while we had the opportunity.

'Vinnie was only starting her fence-walking when I left her,' I said. 'Everyone else is out for the day.'

'Good,' she said for the third time. I took her hand and led her into the bedroom where I'd slept that night. The room was still dim, as I hadn't opened the drapes. The bed was mussed with sheets lying as I'd left them, ready for a return to bed.

I considered what we were about to do and heard myself ask: 'Should we let this happen?'

Marnie's response was succinct. 'How can it be wrong?'

I took her in my arms and kissed her. She unbuttoned my shirt and pulled it back over my shoulders and off my arms. I knew I smelled musky at best. She didn't seem to mind. In a few moments more we were both in less clothing, embracing again, fitting together as we quickly became accustomed to each other's particular anatomy.

After a shower, I made a pot of tea. We were on our second cup when Vinnie returned. She looked appreciative to find hot tea at the ready. She seemed glad as well to have a paying customer. Or was her pleasurable smirk a response to seeing Marnie and me together?

Soon enough we drove back to Marnie's apartment. Before walking the remaining few yards to Jamie and Alice's, I stopped for a while inside her flat.

'I want to thank you again. For picking me up today. And for getting the boat and helping me scatter the ashes. And . . .'

'My pleasure.'

I looked into her welcoming eyes and realised that we were on the verge of something – of departing forever, or of stepping closer. Her breathing, like mine, was growing noticeably deeper. Until she caught her breath abruptly and broke the contact.

'You're leaving Tuesday?' she reminded us both.

'Yes,' I said, knowing that we'd let the moment go. 'Belfast tomorrow. Then, yes, back to America on Tuesday.' I hoped my voice sounded normal. Inside I was whimpering. 'Back to work. Technically I was on a leave of absence.'

'You were working most of time you were here!' she protested.

'Well, yes,' I conceded. 'Not really every day.'

'No.'

We couldn't decide what to say next, how to keep the conversation light, if we wanted to. I stood watching her. She was looking out the window, not really giving her attention to anything in the landscape.

'Will you come back some day, do you think?'

I hoped to come back. I might have to. I could leave all the business about the house in Robbie's hands, but I shouldn't. I should settle my own affairs. My own affairs. Oh yes, I would be back for sure. That's what I'd been telling myself lately. Yet, thinking about it now, I was afraid that returning here would be too painful.

'I don't know . . . I mean yes. I don't know when. I don't know for how long.'

She nodded quietly. When she turned to face me, she managed a little smile. 'I'm sure we'll meet again. If you're around.'

'I hope . . . Yes, we will. I . . .' I didn't have anything else to say.

'It's all right,' she said, 'what happened between us. I'm not going to apologise for what I've been feeling these past few days, and I don't think you should either. I don't want to know about the future. I think I . . . What I'm feeling now will sustain me, for quite some time.' Her smile faded. 'We should say goodbye now.'

The critical moment between us had passed. Without resolution. We'd backed away from the brink. Now it was time to go. I extended my hand.

She took my hand in hers. She drew me close to her for a kiss. And a second one before we parted. I was disinclined to let go.

She withdrew her hand and backed a step away.

'Time to go, Tom,' she said softly.

I didn't want to go away. I forced myself to walk to the door, open it and step across the threshold.

'Have a safe trip back to America,' she said.

The door was closed, with me on the outside and our hands a mere door's thickness apart. 'Goodbye, Marnie,' I whispered.

17

COME TO THE OCEAN

From Marnie's apartment I returned to my uncle's B & B and another tea. I repacked the clean clothes I never had the chance to change into. I hadn't spent a single night there, I was sorry to realise. It wasn't fair, part of my mind complained. I answered myself that it didn't matter, I'd spend more time with Uncle Jamie's family on another trip. One more reason to come back.

But suddenly that rationale was not good enough. My personal life had been kept on hold for decades while I told myself that I'd get around to doing this or that sometime later. My career might have been going great in the interim, but my home life consisted primarily of solitary, insignificant passages of time. Maybe I needed to take time to stop and smell the coffee. The flowers.

And so I was anxious to return to my own little house in Magilligan while I could, to enjoy the few hours I had left there, even though I also wished I could spend more time with Jamie and Alice. And Marnie.

Just a few hours later I returned from the Moville McDermotts' territory into the company of the Magilligan cousins. After dinner at Robbie's – sombre due to my own quiet mood – we retired to the kitchen. The kitchen table – the family office. I handed over outstanding bills from the house to Robbie – to Jane really, as the family's accountant – and I set up a plan to reimburse what they paid out. Since I'd be leaving for Belfast the next day, I gave Robbie and Jane extra keys for both the house and the car. Turning over the keys reminded me poignantly of the earlier transaction, less than a fortnight ago, when Jane had handed Dad's keys to me.

When our business at Robbie's was finished and I declined a final strone of tea, I said my goodbyes to the McDermotts in County Derry. Tomorrow they'd be long gone off to school or to work before my taxi came. The fact that Jane and Robbie trusted me to my own resources was a good sign. They weren't treating me like the stranger I was when I first arrived. Besides, I was only going to the Bellarena station to catch a train to Belfast.

The sky was darkening, the air piercingly cold when I drove back to Dad's house. I was glad to get inside where it was cosy. Cosier when I lit a fire and put on a Rachmaninoff recording, wondering what Rachy would make of CD technology. Instead of packing, I wandered through the house, looking through all the rooms, convinced that there was some significant memento I might take with me. I couldn't, though. I couldn't take away what belonged here, not a single photo.

Nothing left to do then until morning. I fixed myself a drink, pouring a customary two-fingers' measure of whisky – a liquor I'd grown quite fond of recently – and brought it into the study where the turf fire was steadily burning.

Dad was there, in his chair, motionlessly listening to the

music. He looked older, like when I'd last seen him alive.

'You're quiet tonight,' I observed.

'Pensive, I suppose.'

'Why is that? Shouldn't your mood be steady, regular – now that you're dead? I mean, what can change?'

He grimaced. 'There's a theory that you carry all your baggage – the unfinished business, as some would have it – with you when you die. What's in the baggage is whatever troubles, whatever good times you've packed.'

'What are your troubles tonight?' I asked.

He didn't answer directly. 'Another theory you might not like is that, as a mere figment of your imagination, I must necessarily reflect what's going on in your mind.'

I thought about that.

'You're right,' I finally said. 'I don't care for that theory at all.' Already the people I'd met in Ireland, the land, this house, the ocean air, the smell of burning turf were joining Dad as ghosts in my mind. I refused to reduce them to the status of figments.

I looked out at the night-time landscape – cold, desolate and familiar. I sipped at the whisky. Breathed in the fire's fragrance. I walked through the house, looking at the furnishings, old and new, at the photos scattered here and there. When I had my fill, I returned to the study and sat in the rocking chair.

'Was it like this?' I asked. 'When you left?'

'It was warmer then . . .'

I shook my head. 'The feeling, I mean. Did it feel like this? . . . Like you were dying before your time?' If anyone knew what that felt like, he would.

I knew his answer before he spoke it. I heard an old sadness in his voice.

'Yes.'

I expected Dad to ask me for a whisky, to spend our last few moments together drinking in near silence. Instead he rose from his chair. He spoke gently.

'Come with me, Tom. Come to the ocean.'

Under a dark, new moon, I followed the ghost of my father out through our garden and down the quiet road. Once we were passed by a car. Blinded by its lights, I stumbled into the verge, scratching myself on prickly gorse.

'Whin bush,' my dad said without turning. 'It grows most everywhere.'

We walked on until we were in the dunes – at the beach, the strand. I say 'in' the dunes because that was how our location felt to me. We walked between the hills' heights, in valleys lying hidden and protected by the higher mounds. The dunes were covered with bent – feet-long blades of untamed grass, laid over by their own weight, so that my feet were buried in inches of flattened, thick, wet grass.

'Here,' he said, gesturing broadly about himself. 'Here is where I died. I thought it best you see it before you go. Close out the story, you might say.' As though closure could be that easy.

I joined him atop a sand hill.

'Here's as far as I got,' he said. We were facing the ocean. The dunes continued on a few yards before giving way to the sandy beach. 'It was a day or so short of the full moon that night. Ebb tide. The beach was broad, glistening in the moonlight.'

He turned away from the ocean and led me back into a flat, low spot among the dunes. When I stepped down into the tiny valley, I was out of the worst of the cold, although I could still feel and hear the breezes stirring the sand and whistling through the foliage.

'It wasn't at all painful,' he continued, answering a question I hadn't asked, lest the answer be unpleasant. 'I was on a slow walk. Don't know what brought me out. Suddenly I was overcome by fatigue; I couldn't catch my breath. I had to lie down. So I lay here. And the pain stopped.'

'Were you thinking about phoning for help?'

'You mean the call you received?' He shook his head. 'No. I wasn't focused on telephones at all. I didn't feel I was in distress. I was just having a comfortable lie-in, though I knew I was dying ... I did think it would be nice to hear your voice again, as I was fading out.'

I looked about us. The area was unrevealing. No signs that a man had lain here, had died here, had been inspected and removed by police trampling about less than a fortnight ago.

'Seems a good place for repose,' I commented, not knowing what else to say. The site did not close out any story for me. I wasn't in a frame of mind to accept endings.

'Did you know this was a graveyard?' he asked in a lighter tone. He'd taken a seat on the dewy ground.

'No,' I answered. I sat beside him, knowing that surely this must be the precise spot where he died. 'You're serious?'

'You won't find it listed anywhere,' he said. 'It's not recorded officially. But the older people around here know. Some two, three hundred years ago – longer, perhaps – the dead from shipwrecks or from ships in sight of land were often buried just above the shoreline. At that time in Ireland, Christians were buried lying west to east, so their eyes would be facing east for the second coming of Christ. Did you know that?'

'No.'

'A body was found here when I was a boy,' he continued matter-of-factly. 'Some of the bones were exposed. Gave the locals a bit of concern until the bones were identified as being well over a hundred years old. Could have been a foreign sailor – he was buried north to south.'

'And what about you? How were you lying when you were found?'

He looked down at the ground under us. 'Northwest to southeast, I should think.' He gave a small laugh that made me smile.

I leaned back against a damp, grassy dune. The seat of my trousers was already wet through with dew. It didn't matter.

I fingered a flowerless plant at my side. 'Rosemary?' I asked.

'Nae,' he responded. 'Lady's bedstraw. Some people mistake it for whin, at a distance. It would have yellow flowers earlier in the year.'

Yellow. At the edge of my consciousness I recalled the faded yellow shirt worn by my dream ancestor, Seán Sylvanus Finney.

My father went on. 'This is purple thyme,' he said, indicating another plant.

Thyme? Was thyme for remembrance? No, I recalled, thyme is associated with death. But didn't the Romans prescribe it to lift the spirits?

'What does it mean, then,' I asked, 'this graveyard for victims of the sea?'

'In itself, nothing.' He gestured around him. 'It's unlikely any of our family were buried here. Quite possible that no one from Magilligan has ever been buried here. Like you said, it's a graveyard for victims of the sea – not those who died from natural causes, from famine, from war or the troubles.' He sighed. 'Still, it's part of it all – part of this land, my life here, our heritage. Doesn't mean anything outside that.'

And now this mysterious, unregistered graveyard had become part of my life, just the tiniest little chapter in my story. These poor briny buggers were interred here to be integrated into the soil where the greater half of my bloodline was rooted. Part of it all.

Dad left me a bit later. He'd been sitting beside me, resting against the dune – could it be a fairy mound? – then he was gone. He left me calmed by the visit to his resting place. My problems, my conflicts felt less burdensome for a while.

My walk home was solitary. I was cold, but not likely to catch my death of pneumonia.

Back in the house, I immersed myself in the peace and comfort of home. Clear-headed, untroubled, I lay in my bed, in my house, enjoying the night. It was nothing like the apartment in Hull, where I kept the windows closed against noises, pollen and pollution. Here, through a window ever so slightly ajar, I heard the breath of an occasional breeze – accompanied by the faint, steady background roll of the near-distant ocean. A light scent of burnt turf drifted in from the opposite end of the house. I lay pondering the implications of genetic memory versus my own life's experiences. It was an old argument: When you're overwhelmed with the knowledge of a place, are the supernatural sensations you feel true psychic experiences or the ghosts of history?

I lay watching the deepening levels of black until the darkness overtook me and my eyes closed.

18

A COLD DAY IN THE NORTH

I awoke early, after a dreamless sleep. The peaceful night had given way to a restless morning. I was miserable company. Thankfully I didn't need to talk to anyone yet. I faxed a note to Jack at *Heights*, letting him know when I'd be returning. I copied personal papers I thought I might need and transferred my work files from the computer onto floppy diskettes. I washed the dishes, cleaned the bathroom, vacuumed, changed the bed linen. My first stabs at packing were interrupted by television, by the mail delivery, by a desperate need for tea. I tried a few radio stations before playing a CD instead. The exquisitely executed Bach fugue irritated me; I turned it off.

Finally I gave up the idea of packing, grabbed my car keys and headed out east on the Seacoast Road. On impulse I turned in at Downhill House for another walk among the ruins to suit my mood. Today the place wore the forlorn look of an abandoned lover. The sky was dark and the wind bitter, slinging the rain that had held off until now. I should have worn a sweater under my light coat. I was shivering. For relief from the stinging wind, I stepped into an interior turn of a house wall, where I could look out through a windowless opening – to the west, to a small stretch of cliff, to Magilligan, to Donegal, to the constant ocean. The cold bit my eyes.

I stood there, gazing through the scenery – plotting out the houses and pubs I knew in Magilligan, as surely as if I had x-ray vision to penetrate the hills between – until I caught myself humming 'St James Infirmary'.

I finally realised that the cold rain had penetrated my jacket; I was chilled to the bone. I wished I was home, down in the valley, in my bungalow. Warmed by a turf fire. Playing the sturdy piano, or listening to music on the radio, on CD, on tape. Or working at the computer. Or cooking dinner. Or talking to a new friend, a good friend. Or . . .

No time to enjoy a proper fire when I returned home. I finally finished the packing, finding, to my amusement, that Walker had left his soiled shirt behind. When the taxi came to pick me up, I locked the house, glad to know that Jane and Robbie would be looking after things. Nevertheless, I found comfort in holding on to my own set of keys.

Well, this is it, I thought, when I'd been deposited by the solitary platform at the tiny old Bellarena train station. The end of my mystical journey. I didn't expect to see anyone I knew, so I was surprised when a car pulled off the road and its driver approached me. Harley Tennent.

'Inspector,' I greeted him.

'Mr McDermott. I thought it was you standing there.' He looked at the luggage I was carrying. 'Leaving for America?'

'Tomorrow. Belfast today.' I wondered what he was doing there. 'Are you on duty?'

He didn't answered my question.

'Your father seems to have been well liked, Tom,' he said. 'I'm sorry I never got to meet him.'

I bit my tongue to keep from saying that he might likely encounter Dad still hanging around; we weren't far from my home. 'Thanks.'

'We'll keep an eye on the house for you,' he offered.

'Thanks,' I said again. 'Jane and Robbie will be checking on it from time to time as well.

He smiled. 'It's good you've seen to that.'

Something just occurred to me. 'Is Magilligan part of your patch?'

'Oh, yes. It's all part of the Borough of Limavady. It's the quiet corner actually. Very little terrorism up this far north.'

'Compared with Limavady itself, you mean?' I asked, somewhat surprised, because of course I'd seen no terrorist activity at all during my short, peaceful stay.

'Limavady, yeah. And even more so in Dungiven.'

'Really? I had no idea.' I thought about it a moment. 'I'm lucky then to be up here by the coast. In the midst of desolation.'

'You don't like the quiet?' he asked.

'Not at all. I mean, yes, I do like the quiet. When I say it's desolate, I say it with . . . appreciation. You must know what I mean, Inspector. I take it you spend a good amount of time up here.'

He nodded once, just barely. 'Not on official business.'

At last I got another admission of sorts from Inspector Harley Tennent. Besides being friendly with my cousins, he was a frequent visitor to Magilligan, and not in his official capacity. Did he have other business interests in the area?

Or did he have a romantic draw to Magilligan? Not improbable. Now there was a mystery I wasn't likely to solve during my last few minutes in the northwest. Another bit of unfinished business for later.

For now, my train was pulling in.

19

'THIS DISTRACTED GLOBE'

The first leg of the train ride took me back up through Magilligan, within sight of my house, past Magilligan's old railway station (now a residence and tourist flat). We crossed and followed the Seacoast Road, running along the strand at Downhill and into the tunnel I'd photographed earlier. There my restlessness ended and I fell into a deep sleep that lasted until we pulled into Belfast.

I grabbed a black taxi at the station and had the driver give me a jumbled tour of Belfast's city centre – the new Waterfront Concert Hall and the Royal Courts of Justice, signs for the BBC studios, the rather grand Grand Opera House on Great Victoria Street, then City Hall opposite Donegall Place, all decorated with early Christmas lights, and an intriguing section of pedestrianised alleyways or 'entries' where many old city pubs were located – more sights to explore another time. Eventually we headed south, towards Queen's University, and the taxi dropped me at the theatre where Walker was in rehearsal.

The director was restaging a scene when I entered. The cast walked through the new blocking a couple of times then broke for tea. Walker introduced me briefly to the director and some of the cast, saying only that I was his American cousin who'd come over for his father's funeral, not mentioning that I was arts and entertainment editor at *Heights* magazine. The break was long enough for me to join Walker and his flatmate, Suzanne, for a ploughman's and drinks nearby, but was too short for Walker to take me to his apartment. Fine, I said. I really wanted to see the rehearsal, if he didn't mind.

He didn't mind in the least. He was actually quite pleased to have an audience. Between mouthfuls of the cold meal, he outlined the plot. Basically, it was a modern romance story – young man and woman fall madly in love, move in together, drift apart as they settle down, have affairs, separate, marry others, and reunite years later with a questionable outcome. Walker was playing the young man, Suzanne the other woman whom he unwisely marries. Tonight's rehearsal was a full walk-through, with adjustments in the blocking to reflect the characters' changing relationships. Back in the theatre I settled myself in the stalls for the duration.

When the rehearsal ended, we walked back to Walker and Suzanne's place, not far from the theatre after all. The apartment was a three-room, first-storey flat in a block-long row off University Street. I'd have the sofa, which was large enough for frequent guests crashing for the night. I offered to pay for a takeaway or even any groceries, but the couple already had the evening's meal planned. They served up salad and a vegetable casserole that only required reheating, while we started on an inexpensive French white wine.

Over the simple, late dinner – *so* New York – we talked about the rehearsal and the director's comments, and my short jaunt from Bellarena.

'Know who I ran into at the station?' I asked. 'Inspector Harley Tennent.'

'Really? And what do you think of him?'

'Strange bird. I can't figure where he fits into the family.'

'Can't you?'

'A romantic tie somewhere?'

'On the nose.'

Interesting. 'With whom?'

'Ellen.'

'Uncle Jamie's daughter? I still haven't met her.'

Walker shook his head. 'Ellen Rafferty. Aunt Hannah's daughter.'

'Oh. That explains why he's so readily welcomed.'

'Don't let appearances deceive you. Much of the family don't like his being around. He is not widely accepted by them.'

'Really? I didn't noticed anyone being rude to him.'

'No? Well, that's Magilligan for you. The people can be stubborn and opinionated, but they mind their manners. And they avoid stirring up trouble ... But in time you'd catch a few negative remarks.'

Suzanne asked: 'Why don't they like this man? Is it the Protestant/Catholic business again?'

'Not as such,' Walker explained. 'The family are mixed religiously, but there's still some resentment to people from the British sector – partially an anti-unionist sentiment, I'm sure, and partially the kind of resentment to "foreigners" that can be found in any country. Harley is actually English, you know; he's only been over here for about six years. And he's RUC.'

'So?' I queried.

'There are a number of reasons why people hate the police. Some are on general principles, some because of the overwhelmingly Unionist or Protestant composition of the force, and some on the basis of purely personal experiences.'

'Would Andy Rafferty be one of the inspector's more vocal adversaries?'

Walker nodded. 'He would be, if he weren't reined in by his family. You see, Harley was involved in keeping Andy out of prison at one point. That's how he got to know the Raffertys. Ever since then Andy's been resentful for the fines he had to pay and for being indebted to the inspector. Meanwhile, Ellen became involved with Harley. And then Aunt Maddy, who's also Andy and Ellen's aunt, gave her approval to the relationship, so the family have officially, if somewhat begrudgingly, had to accept Harley Tennent.'

'Sounds like a soap opera,' Suzanne commented.

'I suppose I'm in the same boat as the inspector,' I said. 'Being an outsider, I mean.'

'Ah, but you're family. If they didn't all like you on your own, they'd accept you as Mickey's son ... You don't feel like an outsider, do you?'

I shook my head. 'I suppose not ... I feel a bit like Hamlet,' I said, as the association sprang into my mind, not for the first time. 'Coming back to the old family home from a life abroad. Instantly immersed in the elements of my father's existence. And his ghost,' I added incautiously, due to the wine and a need to speak freely.

I glanced at Suzanne, wondering how she'd take my mention of the supernatural.

'It's all right.' She waved away my concern. 'I'm used to Walker going on about ghosts and fairies all the time.'

I nodded, acknowledging that she didn't find me strange – well, at least no stranger than Walker. 'Anyway, that's probably the limit of the association,' I concluded.

'How do you mean?'

'The dead king's manifestation. There is the similarity of duty to family as well – Hamlet's duty to his father. In my case, though, no murder. Nothing to avenge. My father's death was completely peaceful. The only turmoil has been in my own head, trying to incorporate this Irish world into my memories of his life.'

'"Remember thee? / Ay, thou poor ghost, while memory holds a seat / In this distracted globe."'

'Exactly.'

'What was he like when you were growing up?'

'Supportive. Very supportive ... Unlike my mother, who tried to convince me to go into law or politics. If she had known that I'd taken the LSAT and the GMAT and all those tests ...'

'L-sat? G-mat?'

'They're tests you take for admission into law school, business school and the like. I didn't know what I wanted for sure. It was not law school though, I decided that. So I went on to graduate school instead – journalism, English – and Mom finally gave up on me. She had to be satisfied that I finally got a real job instead of staying a professional student. But it wasn't like that with Dad. I could talk things out with him. He'd bring up other points of view, but he never pushed. I don't think I ever knew whether he preferred one career path for me over another. He never tried to influence my professional choices, but he supported my decisions ... That's what it's been like growing up with Dad. How about you two?'

Walker grinned. 'Nothing to tell. My parents expected I'd end up performing somehow. It was a foregone conclusion.'

'Same here,' Suzanne added. 'I come from a large family, and my parents were just glad to see us earn our own livings. Not that they begrudged me dance school and the singing lessons.'

I laughed. 'That was one thing Dad did push. He always told me that I should sing more. Not professionally, mind you. For my own enjoyment.' I sighed. 'The one thing I do regret is that he didn't tell me more about his life here.'

'Maybe he was saving it,' Walker offered. 'Or maybe he didn't think you were ready. After all, the goings-on here weren't part of your life.'

'They could have been,' I protested. Then I realised he was right and conceded: 'It may be I wouldn't have understood this world – not from the viewpoint of my own life in America.'

'Will you see his ghost again, do you suppose?'

'I don't know. He doesn't seem to be staying around for the usual reasons – like unfinished business or violent death. I think he's remained simply for the pleasure of it. I imagine he'll continue to roam through Magilligan for as long as he likes.'

It was comforting to think of Dad still hanging around the old house at his leisure. The image was, however, distracting. I was in Belfast now, the guest of my cousin. And Suzanne. I certainly didn't mean to exclude her from our conversation. I found her rather interesting and I thought her career might be worth tracking. She was one of those people you'd likely assume was an actress; she simply looked the part. I asked for her headshot and résumé for my files, if she had copies to spare. (And what actor doesn't?)

'What about mine?' Walker asked.

'Marnie gave me yours,' I reassured him.

'Oh.'

Suzanne asked, 'Who's Marnie?'

Walker looked at me and winked. 'Marnie's a friend of the family. She handles all my public relations in Donegal. She's trying to get Tom to put me in his magazine.'

'You're going back to New York then?' Suzanne asked.

I was struck sober. There must have been some discussion and speculation about me before my arrival. What had Walker said? 'Of course I'm going back. I live there. And I'm quite fond of my work. In fact, I've been on the job most of the time I was over here.'

'Sorry. I was under the impression that . . .'

'I don't think Tom wants to give up his job in New York,' Walker said, trying to modify how he must have explained my circumstances to Suzanne. 'On the other hand, he does have unfinished business in Derry. He's got his dad's house to contend with.'

'Among other things,' I admitted.

'And we won't drag out of you exactly what those other bits of unfinished business are, will we?' he said.

'No, we won't,' I agreed. Not yet.

'Instead,' he said, 'we'll intimidate you into revealing what you really think about the play.'

'No problem there,' I responded. 'Unless you're friends with the author.'

'You don't like it.' Suzanne mugged a pout. 'Is it really so bad?'

'It's harmless enough, I suppose. It'll serve its purpose. Your purpose, I should say.' I sipped my wine. 'Limited run, is it?'

'How do you know that?' she asked with suspicion. Did I know something about the play that she didn't?

'It's obviously a showcase, literally or otherwise, for what's-her-name. The actress playing Susan. Beth?'

'Becky. Becky Donahue. O'Donaghue, for real. Damn!'

Walker understood my reasoning. 'It makes sense. Becky's supposed to be the up-and-coming star of the Belfast stage. She has top billing.'

'I should have realised,' Suzanne complained. She turned to Walker. 'Who's behind the financing?'

I jumped in. 'I wouldn't worry about it if I were you.'

'Why not?'

'I'm sure Becky will get fine reviews. Maybe some that glow a bit.'

'Lovely,' Suzanne grumbled.

'But,' I added quickly, 'she won't have longevity in the

theatre. In the long run, she's not the one who'll benefit most from the run.'

'Who will?' Walker asked.

I looked at him, then at Suzanne. 'Trust my instincts,' I said in response. 'It's my job to know about things like this.' That was a lie. My business was identifying talent and potential, not predicting success. But I was confident they'd both do all right.

20

BACK TO WORK

Wednesday found me back in the apartment in Hull. At three thirty in the morning, I was wide awake, with coffee and a bagel from the all-night doughnut shop. After my flight to the States and the cabs and trains home the night before, I'd fallen into bed totally drained of energy. I couldn't convince my internal clock that it was not really eight thirty in the morning. I also couldn't sleep because my sinuses, my throat and bronchi had already begun swelling from allergies and pollution. And so I had plenty of time to sort through two weeks of mail, make a grocery list and still catch an early train into the city.

In the office, work was an exercise in mechanical tasks – sifting through junk mail (e-mail, voice mail, snail mail), copy-editing, changing and approving lay-outs, returning phone calls – even though Jack had kept up with the work.

Late in the morning Ellie Prosser dropped into my office, surprised to find me.

'What are you doing here? Were we expecting you?'

Yes, I assured her, I had notified the office when I would be back. I thanked her for her condolences and the flowers and the donation the office had sent.

'You could have stayed longer,' she said, to my amazement. I'd been expecting a fabrication of crises that I ought to have been around to handle. 'I was going to ask you to check out the theatre in Belfast. That is in your area isn't it – Belfast?'

'It is.' In truth, Ireland was small enough that any part of the island was within driving distance.

'You remember the spread we just did on Dublin theatres?' The issue probably went out two years ago. 'Just did' to Ellie meant any time within memorable history. 'We need to keep our eye open for something similar for Belfast. I keep hearing the theatre there is on the rise. I have no idea what they're actually doing – local material, classics? I thought you could go check out some plays, get to know some of the people in the industry. Keep an eye out, you know – your usual sort of thing. Back-burner work. We need to establish connections there.'

I shook my head in amusement. 'I already have contacts in the Belfast theatre,' I said, meaning, of course, my very own cousin Walker. How ironic could my life be?

'Do you now?' She squinted at me. 'Have you gone psychic on me again?' That was her standard accusation whenever I anticipated some new project. 'Well, why don't you rough out a plan of action and we'll talk about it next week.'

As she started to walk away, I called after her. 'Aren't you going to say you missed me, Ellie?'

'I only missed you when Jack wouldn't let me get through to you, Tom.'

'He was following my instructions.'

'Of course,' she harrumphed.

'Didn't our partnership work?' I asked with false naivety.

'It worked all right,' she conceded. 'The two of you make a pretty good team – in spite of everything.'

We did make a good team at that. Jack in the office, me in the field and working from home. I began to wonder . . .

I broached the subject with Jack over lunch – a late lunch for him, an early dinner for me.

'How was our working arrangement for you, when I was away?'

'To tell the truth, great,' he answered. 'I had more responsibility, a lot more responsibility. More hands-on involvement. You know – things that people would normally come to you for if we were both here. Deferring, as they should, to your position and your experience,' he added with a wink. 'I got to make decisions for a change.'

'You didn't mind being stuck in the office all day?'

'Mind? No. You know I don't like being on the road too much. I'd rather stay in the office, have standard hours, and get home for dinner with my family.'

Yes, I did know that already. I sipped at my coffee, delaying long enough to plan my wording.

'I've been mulling over an idea, Jack. That I might spend more time in the field. Maybe something like the way we've been working the past couple of weeks. I haven't said anything to anyone yet,' I added hastily, 'especially not Prosser. I'd have to figure out how to propose any kind of change in our positions.' I paused for the idea to take hold. 'What's your initial reaction?'

He considered the plan. 'It could work. As you say, we'd have to iron out the details before presenting it to Ellie. I'd be willing to try something like that, if you're serious.'

I was serious. And yet I didn't want to seem too eager to push an arrangement that might not fly with *Heights* management. 'At this point it's all idle thinking on my part. We can talk again later.'

'Sure.'
'Next week maybe?'

Hours later the workday was over and I was alone in Hull. In the late afternoon, before the sun had sunk in resignation below the horizon – the pre-twilight time I always hated – I took a few blocks' walk downtown to the river. I looked at the Hudson River and thought of the northern Atlantic Ocean. Hull-on-Hudson was a worn-down town. Its economy had seen far better days. Hull was quiet and isolated. Very much like Magilligan. And yet not at all the same. It didn't feel the same at all.

Back in the apartment, I poured myself a dram of whisky, which I sipped from time to time, sniffing the smoky aroma. I put off unpacking. Instead, I sat down to look at the Ireland pictures I'd had processed while I was at work.

I took the two packets from my briefcase and began flipping through the prints. As I lingered over each one, my thoughts drifted out of grasp. Eventually I admitted that I couldn't deal with them. Maybe at the weekend I'd feel like putting them in some sort of order, sticking them in an album and labelling them. In the meantime, I put them back into the packets and left them on the desk. The desk, in fact everything in the apartment, still looked like motel furniture. I didn't know why I hadn't replaced everything years ago. Or perhaps I did know. The truth was that I always thought of the apartment as a temporary residence rather than a home.

Bugger it all, I thought to myself. Work, I could handle fine; I knew where I stood. What unsettled me was unfinished business in my personal life, where I didn't know the likely outcome.

I tried distracting myself a while longer. I retrieved my travel jeans from the bedroom floor and dug into the pockets. I dropped handfuls of Irish and British currency into my money dish on the dresser top. I felt suddenly very tired. Jet-lagged. Must be. I should have stayed up, forced myself back into the rhythm of this time zone. I should have, but I was too tired and drooping in spirit to re-acclimatise.

I dragged through the following day (which again began ridiculously early) and the day after that. Nothing out of the ordinary in the office. Every evening came quickly and found me soon back in the apartment not wanting to do any of the simple tasks waiting for me. Thanksgiving was around the corner, I knew, because of all the reminders at work and a call from my mother to make sure I was coming to her house as promised. I did vaguely recall that she had committed me to come after I'd spent some other major holiday – was it the Fourth of July? Bastille Day? Labor Day? – at Sharon's house instead of hers.

21

A QUEST FOR THANKSGIVING

Time moved on – another week, then the next. Except for relapses on weekends, I was making progress readjusting to New York time.

The first Saturday home, I had screwed up my curiosity and gone to a local church's Celtic Christmas crafts show. I was half looking for a recording by an artist I'd heard on radio in Ireland. I didn't find it among the dozens of bright-green-labelled recordings by the singers who rendered what were considered to be Irish standard tunes – 'I'll Take You Home, Kathleen' and that ilk. I saw plenty of "Tis Himself' and "Tis Herself' sweatshirts, cotton/polyester handkerchiefs with bold green shamrocks machine-sewn on, leprechaun dolls and leprechaun-decorated boxer shorts, 'Kiss me, I'm Irish' T-shirts, shamrock ties and pins, tin whistles, calendars of Irish castles, expensive handknit sweaters and factory imitations, New Age video tours of Ireland, collectible ceramic cottages and Fighting Irish banners. I passed by a gathering of middle-aged men with bulging beer guts, red, broken-veined noses. I heard a painful, exaggerated accent that is probably nonexistent anywhere in Ireland but is considered, in the States, a quaint 'brogue'. I'm sure these were all very good people, but I knew I'd never fit into their community. I left the crafts show quickly, empty-handed.

I plodded through the days, spending as much time as I could at work. I eventually unpacked my clothes, did laundry, dropped off shirts (including Walker's that I'd forgot to return) at the dry cleaner's one Saturday and picked them up the following weekend. When I checked my dry-cleaned jacket, I found traces of sand still in the pockets; the sea shells were piled on the dresser.

On Thanksgiving Day I intended to arrive as early as I could at Mom and Carl's. I owed Mom a private talk about Dad before Carl's family arrived; I supposed I owed her the opportunity for what she'd call closure and what I considered an epilogue to my parents' life together. I didn't relish discussing McDermott family business with the Weaver clan. That was the plan. However, my delay over breakfast and the newspaper's crossword puzzle, aided by highway congestion, determined the time of arrival, scarcely a quarter of an hour before the others were expected.

Having a caterer in to actually cook the Thanksgiving meal freed up Mom's time, but didn't alleviate her annoyance with everyone. Carl's brother Bob would be coming but his other brother Henry and Henry's wife, Fran, had decided at the last minute to spend the weekend skiing instead of suffering through the long drive to Scranton. Mom thanked God her own family (the new set, I assumed) would be present. She wondered aloud, before the meal was even finished cooking, what on earth she'd do with all the leftovers.

Still in all, Mom was not frazzled. She was, in fact, the picture of the cool, sophisticated suburban businessman's wife to which she'd always aspired. Her complaints were driven more by nature than by emotion. She wore a simple pearl necklace and earrings and a dress of cream-coloured, textured fabric. Her hair, a shade lighter than when I'd last seen her, was precisely coiffed to bounce loosely without losing shape.

'Was it a nice funeral?' she asked out of the blue. 'Do you think I should have flown over?'

I shook my head. 'No one expected you. I mean, with the divorce so long ago.' I added an afterthought I knew she'd want to hear. 'Dad's family did ask after you, though. How you were.'

'That's nice. There were a lot of people, I'm sure?' She was relaxing now, forgetting about the diminished number of guests expected for her gathering.

'Quite a good number, actually. His brothers, of course, and numerous cousins — even several times removed. From three counties, I believe. Maybe four. And a lot of local people he'd either known before or met after he came back. He led a quiet life there, but Dad was apparently quite popular.'

Her smile looked a bit strained. Fortunately, for her, any further discussion of her late ex-husband's popularity was interrupted by other players entering the stage.

'Speaking of dads,' she said, rising from her precise ankle-crossed pose on the sofa, 'here's Carl now.'

Carl of the slicked-back grey-white hair of longish length for a conservative. Carl who looked like the staid, low-level financial services vice president he'd always been and always would be (whether in grey/brown two-piece suit or knit shirt and red leisure trousers as now). Carl was the master of the house in which I'd lived the last of my teenage years before defecting to a college dorm.

'Tommy,' he greeted me. 'How's our boy doing?'

'How are you?' I responded shaking his hand. Because of Mom's objection to my calling him Carl and my own refusal to call him Dad, I generally never called him anything.

'Can't complain. Well, I could, but nobody would listen. Ha.' That was Carl. He projected the right image, knew the harmless clichés. No substance whatsoever. 'And look who I found at the airport.'

'Hi, Bob,' I said, shaking Carl's brother's hand. Bob was an accountant. A bit dull, one would expect, yet far more human and likeable than Carl. And unfortunately downtrodden. His wife was a real-estate agent who was frequently and inexplicably out of town on business trips. All the Weavers had suspected for a long time that she was having a string of affairs with other men. Whether or not it was true, even Bob stopped creating excuses for her absences. 'She's away' was the extent of his explanations. I liked Bob's low-key complacency – when he wasn't drawn into number-crunching dialogues with Carl.

'Good to see you, Tom. I'm sorry about your dad.'

'Thomas was just telling me about Michael's funeral,' Mom told Carl. 'You were saying something about his will, I think?'

Well, yes, I was. In our phone conversation a couple of weeks earlier, not now. Mom wasn't expecting Dad to leave her anything, but she hoped for any little acknow-ledgement of their marriage and the years they'd spent together – not entirely unhappily. Although she hadn't been mentioned in it, I promised to bring a copy of the will. I retrieved the papers from the breast pocket of my coat.

'There's not really much to it,' I said. 'You're welcome to have a look.'

'I'm sure it's much too technical,' Mom said as she took the document and handed it over to her husband. 'This is more in your line of work, dear.'

Carl scanned the document through the bottom half of his bifocals. His response was: 'Hmmph. Not much to it is right. Bob?' The papers again passed hands.

After a quick perusal, Bob said: 'Neatly done. A smart man, your dad.' In answer to Mom's quizzical look, Bob continued. 'There are a few gifts to his brothers. Whatever's left in the estate – the bulk – goes into an existing trust. There's nothing to dispute in the will's terms. No details at all; the disposition is handled through the trust. And the trust can't be challenged because it's not a public record.' He handed the papers back to me.

Not that Mom would have dreamed of challenging the will or tried to grab a portion of Dad's estate. Still, I knew she was curious – about how wealthy Dad might have become since the divorce, about how much money she'd abandoned when she left him and married Carl. 'So everything Michael had goes into this trust?' she asked.

'According to his solicitor,' I said, 'there's very little left for probate. Dad had put most everything he owned into trust some time ago.'

'And what happens with this trust? Where does it go?'

I coughed, trying to mask my embarrassment. 'Seems it's all mine,' I answered. 'I never knew. For the last couple of years, from when Dad set up the trust, he administered it for my benefit. Now Uncle Robert's in charge.'

'Michael's brother Robert? But he's even older than . . .'

'Cousin Robbie is the next designated trustee. Between the two of them, they've got everything in order. They're taking care of the house, the bills. Keeping excellent accounting records – no erasures or smudges,' I added for Bob's amusement.

Mom digested the information in silence. Her disposition changed beneath a stony exterior – from polite disinterest to annoyance with Dad for hiding the details of his wealth through a trust, annoyance with the two Robert

McDermotts for having irreproachable power of trustee over that wealth, annoyance with me for not providing extensive details of the trust's holdings. She was also disgruntled by Bob's enthusiasm over the well-structured estate.

Thanksgiving dinner itself was a mixture of drudgery and sublimity. During the grace, the rote pre-dinner blessing, I remained silent under my mother's cold glare. Bob was pleasant company through the meal; having little to say beyond remarks about the weather and his flight, he kept silent. Carl was still Mr Business Man, maintaining what I was convinced was a façade of competence and respectability. Was he good at his job, I wondered, or had he advanced simply by playing the game and posing no discernible threat to his superiors? Mom's blatantly contrived attempts to draw the group into mutual conversation by tossing out topical but non sequitur remarks fell flat. Many people, myself included, truly liked Mom, but they would hardly describe her as the salt of the earth. She couldn't count on natural charms to keep a group engaged in talk.

The dinner table included Mom's second attempt at a family. John – John Carl Weaver – was Mom and Carl's first joint effort, born a few months after the new marriage. As a teenager, I'd avoided Baby John because, I'm sure, my instincts were telling me he'd turn into a nasty bit of work. Now a teenager himself, he was a would-be headbanger, a pseudo-heavy-metallist unable to sing, play an instrument or probably even turn on an amplifier. His look was affected grunge. As though his uncontrolled acne were insufficient adornment, his head was swiss-cheesed with holes made for piercings that Mom wouldn't let him keep. His upper left arm was discoloured from the attempted removal of a tattoo. To his credit John had mastered the unintelligible grunt: I couldn't tell whether his participation in grace was the traditional wording or an incantation for satan's demons to impose hell's fires upon our ensemble.

Theresa Weaver, the sister, was still *in utero* when I'd departed the blissful household. Terry's greatest contribution to the dinner conversation was her whining critique of the sweet potato pie. 'I'm sure I'm not eating any of that. It's, like, gross.' Compared to Terry and John, Sharon and I were model adolescents. Well, perhaps not model, yet surely more palatable than this obnoxious pair.

Fortunately the meal compensated for the company. I had once seriously contemplated disowning my mother for the racial cliché of hiring a black woman to cook for her. The truth of the matter was that Emma Bernhardt was a local caterer whom Mom was quite lucky to get for what turned out to be a rather small family dinner. We'd known Emma for years and I'd gone to school with her daughter, Louisa. At least Bob had the good sense and Mom the graciousness to give the excellent dinner its due and to compliment Emma profusely. At the end of the meal, before the adults adjourned to the living room for after-dinner drinks and television, Emma gave me a nod to come into the kitchen.

'You've outdone yourself, Emma,' I said, taking her hand.

'How are you fixed for pies? I've got extra, with this small crowd.'

'What kind?'

'Pecan.'

'Bourbon?'

'That's a secret I won't tell you. It's something other than bourbon. The pie's yours, if you want it; it's already on your mother's order and she won't be needing it.'

'Sure, I'll take it. But I'll pay you separately. If Mom doesn't scrutinise the bill with a magnifying glass, Carl will.'

'I know how it is,' Emma laughed. 'I've got my own penny-pinching bookkeeper. Guess there's no getting away from family.'

After stashing the pecan pie in my car, I took my leave of the Weavers. John and Terry had disappeared to their own rooms or to the streets – or, more likely, the mall. Bob and Carl were settled in for snoozing through football games. Mom wanted to 'rest' (nap) before starting work on her Christmas card list – an elaborate project, I can attest, involving a detailed system for judging the potential recipients and rating their worthiness. I was released for the long drive home and a good sleep before rerunning the trek the next day.

22

REASONS TO BELIEVE

Just short of noon the next day I was back in Scranton – this time at Sharon's. I gave her Emma's pecan pie, heavy with the undisclosed liquor.

'Great,' she enthused. 'We'll have it after the pizza.'

That was Share at her typical best. She'd certainly have turkey leftovers through the following week, but she had promised the kids they could have pizza for dinner Friday night. And if I brought pecan pie, then there was no question that pecan pie was a perfect complement to pizza. I couldn't help loving her ease and accommodation, and I felt immeasurably closer to her than to our hideous half-siblings, John and Terry.

'The kids call her Teary,' Sharon confessed.

'And John?'

'They've pretty much outgrown calling him Spotty,' she said. I nearly spurted soda through my nose in a laugh. She went on. 'I think they've settled on Lem for now.'

'Lem?'

She threw up her hands. 'Don't ask me. I can only guess they picked it up from something on TV.'

We were in Sharon's kitchen, making a lunchtime dint at the leftovers with gigantic turkey-and-homemade-bread sandwiches. Not a bad cook, Share. She was great at this mom business. Lucy, the quiet, quizzical, lovable little mutt underfoot, agreed with wagging tail as she snatched a morsel of meat from Sharon's fingers. Lucy always made me recall our old dog Woody; now she also brought to mind Brimstone, Kieran's blue-eyed shelty.

At Share's insistence, I reported all the details of my first journey ever to Ireland. The family and all the other people I met. The funeral. ('I hardly expected that my first ceilidh would be at my father's funeral.') The house. My impressions of the country. I even told her about Dad's ghost.

'He was sitting there in the house? Right in front of you?'

'Sitting. Walking. Drinking and talking. Everything short of singing – I suppose another time . . .'

'Huh,' she exhaled. 'How about that? And your cousin says he saw him too?'

'Walker. Yes, more or less.'

'Well,' she said, rising from the table to wash up our sandwich plates. 'You'll have to give old Mick my regards next time you run into him. Tell him he's in my thoughts.'

'Thanks.' I knew she'd never doubt me.

'Now about this woman . . .'

'Marnie?'

'Um-hmm. What is it about her you like so much?' I hadn't admitted feeling anything about Marnie.

'I don't know. She's not put-on. She's her own person, but she seems to get along with everyone. She's probably a very good teacher. She reads people really well and knows how to establish a rapport.'

'You did kiss her at least?'

'Yes. At the very least.'

'And?'

'And what?'

'How did you two get along? Will you ask her out again?'

'On a date other than for ash-strewing? I don't know. I don't know when I'll be there again.'

Share gave me her wise look. 'You'll manage it somehow.'

While we were emptying the dishwasher of the dishes from the previous night's feast, Sharon's husband, Chuck Wrigley (an excellent baseball-sounding name, I always thought), came home with the kids – Jennifer, Alison and George, in descending age order. They'd been out on a scouting expedition, to decide where they'd buy their Christmas tree when it was 'ripe' (as George said). Chuck took over helping Sharon so I could go outside with the kids and play a low-key version of kick-the-can in which no one but old-timer me could get hurt. Then we alternated between the swings and the slide. I was exhausted by the time we finished a game of monkey-in-the-middle with a soft plastic ball and dog Lucy as the monkey. No naps for the kids during this four-day holiday.

Back inside we three adults had a few beers and caught up on the news while the kiddies watched television cartoons and a children's movie special. We rounded off the afternoon with a few rounds of the Uncle Wiggily Game, which was advanced for young George, condescendingly juvenile for Jennifer as eldest child, and just right for Alison and me.

While I was playing board games on the floor, Sharon and Chuck were looking at the photos I'd taken in Ireland.

'And this is?' Sharon was holding up a picture for my identification.

I looked up from where I was sitting cross-legged on the

floor. 'That is Trevor Finney's fishing boat,' I answered, though I knew she wasn't referring to the boat.

'The woman? Is this Marnie?'

'Marnie Dodd.'

'Pretty. And you're absolutely sure she's not related? Not another cousin somehow? Or a cousin-of-a-cousin or whatever?'

'Yes. No blood relation whatsoever.'

'This is when you were taking out the ashes?'

'We were just coming back. She's holding the empty urn.' I explained to Chuck: 'I emptied Dad's ashes in the ocean.'

'I like that idea,' Chuck said. 'Maybe Share can dump me in the Lackawanna River when it's my time.'

'Sure. I'll pencil it in for next weekend,' Sharon kidded him.

I identified the next shots as she held them up. Stretches of coastline, Moville, Greencastle. 'More family. After dinner we all met up for a few drinks. A full evening of drinking, I should say. That's Jamie and Alice McDermott. Trevor and Declan Finney. Trev's wife, Maureen. The boys' mom, Vinnie. The redhead's a more distant cousin – Kieran Finney.'

She paused on the snapshot. 'Hmm. Something about him looks . . . like somebody from another century?'

'I know. He's definitely an old soul in the reincarnation business. Carries genes from the most ancient Finney lines.'

'Oh yeah. The "gentry", right?'

'Right.' In an aside to Chuck I explained about the gentle people, the 'fairy folk' as I thought of them alliteratively.

'Hmm. And this handsome fellow?' She was holding up the separate eight-by-ten glossy.

I laughed. 'Walker McDermott, who else? The actor. His résumé's on the back.'

She scanned his résumé and muttered 'impressive' about the scope of his roles to date, then asked whether he had any movies in the offing that she might be able to catch. 'Not yet,' I answered.

A few more photos, then: 'Marnie again.'

'Sorry, yes. The photos are out of order. I took those in the harbour at Greencastle.'

'And she lives by herself?'

'I was only at her place for five minutes.' Share was giving me her I-don't-believe-you look. 'Ten minutes. At the very most.' I added, almost confessing: 'And half an hour alone at the farm house.'

Sharon grinned, satisfied that her intuition was on the mark. 'Have you written to her yet? You are going to, aren't you?'

'I don't think so. I'm not one for letters.' True enough, that. I'm a prolific writer except when it comes to personal letters.

The kids and I finished the game and I went through the remaining photos, identifying the various people and locations. I couldn't help sighing when we came to pictures of the house in Magilligan, missing it already.

After the pizza (one plain, one pepperoni, one kitchen-sink) and pecan pie and ice cream had settled a bit, Sharon went upstairs with the kids for the hour-long task of teeth-brushing and putting on pyjamas. I was called up to read a bedtime story – a tale of goblins from a book I'd once brought back from England. The dear little monsters wouldn't release me from duty until I sang a couple of lullabies and their eyes were sealed closed with fairy dust.

I liked the life Sharon and Chuck had. I liked playing with the kids on their level while maintaining responsibility as an adult for their well-being. I felt I'd like to have my own family, my own kids. When the time was right. For now, I'd settle for a home of my own that felt like home.

★

The following night, after an early, solitary dinner in the apartment in Hull – when did I start referring to it that way? the apartment in Hull? the Hull apartment? – I rang Marnie's number in Moville. I desperately wanted her to be there to talk. I needed to hear a voice from that other world. I needed to hear her voice.

'Marnie? Hello. It's Tom McDermott.'

'Tom? It's good to hear you. How was your flight back to America?'

'Uneventful. How have you been?'

'You know. You know first-hand how quiet it is here.'

'Even with Christmas coming on?' I asked. Already Manhattan was impossible with cars in gridlock and gawking tourist traffic on the sidewalks and in the shops. And I remembered that Belfast had opened its Christmas shopping season when I was there. But then Belfast was a city, far removed from the wilderness of Magilligan.

'We don't get too riled over the holidays. Over football, yes. But holidays don't have the same build-up. Christmas is nice enough, but . . .'

'Relatively quiet.'

'Yes.' She waited. 'Was there a particular reason you called or . . .'

I hadn't thought beforehand about what I wanted to say. My spontaneous excuse was embarrassingly weak.

'I found one of Walker's shirts mixed in with mine when I picked them up from the cleaner's. I thought he might want me to send it on. I didn't think to ask for his mailing address. You wouldn't have it, would you? Or will you be seeing him?'

'You're more likely to hear from him first,' she answered. 'Anyway, you have Walker's address and phone number from his CV.'

Fair enough. She had caught me out. 'You want me to confess that I called just to talk to you?'

'Yes . . . Whenever you're ready to admit it.'

Clever girl.

'Until then,' I said, stalling to amuse her, 'tell me about what you've been doing. What are you teaching right now? How are your students? Do they like you? Do you like them?'

With a short laugh, she complied, telling me everything I asked. In turn, I told her my work had returned to dull routine. Then I described my recent visit to the pre-Christmas Celtic crafts show and my negative impressions.

'I'm afraid I don't make a very good Irish–American,' I said.

She digested my description and agreed. 'No, I can't see you fitting into that role. You do fine among us, though. It may be that we have a simpler idea of what being Irish means over here. Belonging doesn't mean surrendering your individuality. It certainly doesn't mean buying into the hackneyed commercial aspects of Irish culture.'

There was a compliment there somewhere – even if I was reading one into her remarks. Lest I become big-headed, I changed topics.

'I had the pictures developed.' I had laid them out on the table while I was on the phone. 'Some very good shots of you. Would you like copies?'

'Not copies, no,' she said abruptly. Then she added, rather softly: 'Maybe someday I'll look at them all with you.'

I'd turned down the volume on my CD player before phoning, but I could still hear the song that was playing – 'Una furtiva lagrima negl'occhi suoi spuntó . . .' from Act II of Donizetti's *L'Elisir d'Amore*. I shook my head to ward off my visualising a secret tear in her eye.

'I'll leave the photos in my luggage then.' I cleared my throat, trying to maintain a light tone. 'You looked very competent working Trevor's boat. Do you take it out much?'

'I'm a fair hand at that sort of thing. I've grown up with boats.' I could hear the smile return to her voice. 'I hear you have a way with cows.'

I smiled now. 'I've milked a few in my time. It's simply a matter of warming your hands first . . . What's the weather like now? Does it snow there?'

'It snows, yes. Not so regularly to count on. Today the weather's about the same as when you were here. Generally it doesn't get much colder until January, but we did have a couple of cold nights already. I went with Jane over to your house to be sure there was enough heat to keep the pipes from freezing.'

'Everything was all right?' I could picture the house just as I'd left it.

'Oh yes. I made us tea while Jane was checking on things. I didn't think you'd mind.'

'Not at all. I like to think of there being activity in the house, even if it's only tea occasionally.' I liked the image of Marnie and Jane sitting at my kitchen table. 'Can you smell the turf fires in the air?'

'Right now? The smell is pretty much a constant.'

'And can you taste . . .? Never mind, I'm starting to ramble. Must be tired.' I was. Tired, melancholy. 'Say hello to the family for me, if you happen to see anyone.' I wondered whether passing along my greetings might suggest that we had established some sort of relationship. I needn't have worried.

'I'll be glad to give them your regards.'

'Thanks. I'd better go now. Take care of yourself. I miss you.' Was I saying too much?

'If you want to, call again . . . I like the sound of your voice . . . Goodnight, Tom.'

'Goodnight . . . No, wait. Do you bicycle?'

'What?'

'Do you like to bicycle? Do you have a bicycle?'

'Yes to both. It's good for exercise. Or when I don't want to walk or drive. Why?'

'I was thinking of getting one. To use over there.' Actually I was picturing my imaginary bike and hers parked side by side in the garage. Perhaps I could visit in the summer. Or in spring, though even spring was a long, long way off.

'Well, I'll keep my eye open for one, shall I?'

'Yes, thanks, if it's not too much trouble.' I couldn't think of any additional absurdities to extend the conversation. 'Well, I should go now . . . Take care of yourself.'

''Bye, Tom.'

'Goodnight.'

I hung up the phone. My head was filled with Marnie Dodd and Gaetano Donizetti. 'M'ama, si, m'ama, lo vedo, lo vedo.' If she loved me . . . I interrupted my thought and the CD's playing. What was wrong with me, that I was getting mawkish over an opera?

I gathered up the photos and tossed them into an open suitcase, where they'd sit for God knows how long. I couldn't put the pictures into albums as I once thought I might. I couldn't preserve them like that, memorialise them, as though the story they told had ended.

23

FACTORING IMMIGRATION

After my call to Marnie, I went out to an Irish-theme restaurant and bar on the outskirts of Hull. I didn't know anyone there. The longer I stayed, the more I felt out of place. The bartender, an immigrant from Kerry, divided his attention between customers at large and a group of his fellow countrymen, acquaintances from all parts of Ireland who'd become friends living in their own isolated community in America. They seemed to gather most every night in this bar. They talked about football (soccer) a lot. They never talked about moving back to Ireland. The younger they were, the less homesick they seemed while enjoying the adventure of living in America. I once read that, in the present time, only ten per cent of Ireland's emigrants ever return to the old country.

They drank continuously for hours – bottle after bottle of American beer, seldom pints of the Irish brews on tap. Was it the novelty or economy that drew them to American beer?

The more they drank and the larger their groups, the louder they laughed and the more generously they inserted every grammatical form of the word 'fuck' into their speech. Was it bravado? Whistling in the dark?

I wondered, but I didn't dare ask, whether these recent immigrants were aware they'd probably never return home to live, and that, in just a few years, they might be married and raising children who'd never know the experience of growing up on Irish soil.

The diehard Irish-American community at the bar was more depressing to me than the true Irish immigrants. They appeared to be second- and third-generation and middle-aged. They were raised with an undefined impression of being Irish and an understanding that they were expected to act Irish, whatever that might mean. They talked a lot about Ireland and things Irish, not knowing that many of the morose Irish ballads they played on the jukebox were written in America by Americans (or even German immigrants) and that the Irish paraphernalia they bought was manufactured for tourists, not natives. Many of them fully embodied the caricature of the beer-guzzling Celt. They were also regulars at this bar. So much so that anyone's absence for more than one night became a topic of concern among the cohorts.

With the exception of bartenders and waitresses, there was very little interaction between the Irish immigrants and the Irish-Americans. The Americans sometimes tried to saddle up to the immigrants, but there was no real rapport. And I wasn't drawn to either group. As I stood near the door, ready to leave, I took a final look at the people clustered about the bar. I didn't belong with them. I didn't belong to any part of the Hull community.

I left for home − empty, save for the three pints of Guinness, which tasted unexpectedly weak.

★

Sunday evening I had dinner early once again and was sitting in front of the television, trying not to fall asleep, not to revert to Greenwich Mean Time two and a half weeks after leaving Ireland. I wasn't paying attention to the television movie – or film, as my cousins would say. So I let myself wonder about what was happening across the Atlantic. Instead of dreaming it, I let my mind consciously fantasise a return visit to Ireland. I visualised myself catching a night flight and arriving early in the country, treating myself to the expense of a taxi the entire distance from Belfast's Aldergrove Airport to Magilligan. I'd slip into the house, unannounced and unnoticed, as though I'd only been out for the day. No fanfare. I'd see family after a day or two.

In my mind I saw the house as it looked whenever I returned to it. Small, not unattractive. It could definitely use a few trees in the yard. I knew evergreens would grow there; I could ask what else. A terrace in the back would be nice, outside the kitchen. For the many temperate days. Some roses perhaps. Nothing too perfumey. Nothing too showy. After all, the house would never pretend to be an idyllic rose-covered cottage. Or did I mean ivy-covered? And footpaths along the roads would be nice – to facilitate roaming the neighbourhood and visiting local pubs without being splattered by cars racing through. Oh yes, I was thinking long for my home in Magilligan.

I tried turning my train of thought towards the more practical alternative of making the house marketable. In the real world I'd have to do something with it eventually. It couldn't be allowed to fall apart like after my grandmother's death. I could probably sell it. The house was in prime condition with the recent upgrades. I'd have to dispose of the furniture somehow. Was there some distant cousin who'd be interested? Or someone who'd want to rent the house furnished if I decided I couldn't part with it outright?

The phone rang, disturbing my speculation. It was the same ring as always; how could it be any different? But I knew who, what it would be. I stayed in my chair.

'Give it up, Dad,' I said to the unanswered phone. 'Save your energy for some worthier effort. I haven't decided anything yet.'

The phone stopped. I got up, picked up the receiver. As expected, only dead, soundless air. I hung up the receiver and went off to bed.

24

SCHMOOSING

In the three weeks I'd been back in the States I had managed to thoroughly unsettle my life. Among the unfinished business was the proposed restructuring of my working arrangement with Jack. Finally one Wednesday, an otherwise dull and uncontroversial midweek day, I had a chance to pitch my proposal to Ellie Prosser.

'You said yourself that the arrangement worked well when I was away,' I reminded her.

'Jack's not ready to take over everything you do. You've got a certain – God help me for admitting it to your face – a certain finesse.'

'Schmoosing, you mean? I schmoose best on the phone. Or in neutral territory – restaurants, parks, studios, theatres. I don't need to be in the office for that.'

'What about meetings? There are meetings where your presence is essential – budget discussions, long-range planning. You'd have to be here for those. And emergency production meetings. You have to be on-hand for whenever they're called.'

Her opposition was gaining momentum, so I let her cool down for a moment. Plunging in with a response now would heighten confrontation. I took a sip of coffee and leaned back comfortably in her guest chair, crossing one leg over the other before responding with calm confidence.

'We both know nothing happens at those meetings. They're bullshitting sessions. Everyone expresses an opinion, goes off on tangential discourses and nothing is accomplished. The productive work is done after the meetings, and administrative decisions are made behind closed doors before the next meetings. To the extent that we have any relevant input in those meetings, Jack is more than competent. In fact, he's a hell of a lot calmer and more effective in that forum than I am.' I cut her off before she could protest. 'If I'm really, absolutely needed during any of those endless, God-awful planning meetings – which I truly doubt – I can be conferenced in by phone. Better yet, video-conferencing.' I continued: 'As for production meetings *per se* . . .'

Ellie held up her hand to stop me there. She frowned, clearly discomforted by my having anticipated her arguments. Not difficult to do, since I'd had time to work out the plan in my mind; she'd been freshly assaulted with it. Then she smiled, in a way colleagues have described as evil. She'd found a card up her sleeve after all. 'Simon Morrison,' she pronounced with satisfaction.

I shook my head. 'Didn't I handle Si's work all right when I was away?'

'Feh!' she said. 'Faxing changes back and forth is too cumbersome. It takes too much time to have someone decipher your handwritten notes and input the changes.' A bogus argument, since I was the one who deciphered my own handwriting to produce the typed copy. It was true, however, that someone would have to retype the copy if I faxed it in.

'Floppy disks,' I answered. 'E-mail. Articles can be transmitted to me as e-mail attachments, I can edit the document files directly and send them back in final form. Electronically.'

She countered: 'Sounds like too much technology. Sounds expensive – for the company and for you.'

I wasn't prepared to cede any point. I knew the economics. 'Not terribly expensive. And the company can afford the technology – both here and on my end. At the very least the magazine has a moral obligation to support the kind of high-technology and home-office work environments that we've touted as essential in the evolving business world. If we can't do that, where's our credibility?'

'Meaning what?'

'About a year and a half ago. "Home Is Where the Work Is." Barb Epstein's article?' I didn't need to remind Ellie that Barb Epstein was the CEO of a well-respected consulting firm – and a business pal of Ellie's.

She frowned again, saying nothing. She'd run out of arguments for the present. 'You haven't told me why you want to do this,' she said.

I was expecting that particular line of interrogation earlier. Her bringing it up now, however, was an indication that Ellie had got past her initial opposition and might seriously consider the possible consequences of my plan.

'One reason – a secondary motive, I'll admit – is Jack. I like working with him and I don't want to break up our team. But it's time for him to move up.'

'You want to role-reverse? Become his assistant?' she baited me.

'Co-editors, Ellie. That's the plan. Jack the anchor, me in the field.'

'And your primary motivation?'

Ah, that's what I'd been trying to figure out for myself. How to pin it down?

'To be honest, I'm restless. I'm getting stale. I need to be out in the field, in personal contact. I need to travel. I have to be there. Wherever "there" is ... You'll have to admit my interviews in London turned out rather well.'

'I will admit that I thought you were leading up to asking for a bonus over the Melvin Green coup.'

I shook my head. 'My only real effort on that project was the Randy Phillips piece – a damned good article on its own though. It may have opened the door to get to Melvin Green, but the coup will be Jack's article from the interview.'

'In juxtaposition to your write-up.' She was baiting me again.

I nodded. 'Of course. But the bonus I'll be expecting is for the Katie Halberstadt piece. Artsy presentation, I'll admit, but at the end of the day it's the prize-winner.' Since Prosser had introduced the matter of a bonus, I was not about to let it slip away.

'Didn't you convince me that the genius behind that was the photographer's?'

'Paul Mason. Two geniuses then. You did like the Halberstadt article, didn't you?'

'They were both good articles – Phillips and the one on the actress. You haven't done interviews that good in a long time.'

'Would you say "excellent"?'

'Fine,' – she threw up her hands – 'they were excellent pieces. Outstanding ... Satisfied?'

'Thanks. I wanted the wording right, since I'll be quoting you on that. And, by the way, you've also just admitted that my work has benefited from me being in the field.'

'Damn.'

Poor Ellie.

'Furthermore, remember that you're the one who

brought up the subject of raises.'

'A bonus, not a raise.'

'All right. Since you insist, I'll accept the bonus. The raise can wait until the Halberstadt article actually hits the stands and the issue sells out.' I knew Ellie enjoyed this sort of obvious manipulation – well, to a limit. Although I was close, I hadn't yet reached the limit I had in mind. 'But, as you know, I really came in with a different agenda than the money.'

She sighed.

'All right. Write up your proposal. Give me all the details – what it'll mean as far as workloads, hours, salaries, other expenses. I'll take it under advisement, but you be advised that I have more reservations than I could begin to list right now. Now get out and do some work for the magazine.'

'Thanks, El.' I smiled. Work would wait until after lunch. I'd already made a reservation to take Jack out for a long, drinking meal so we could sketch out a skeletal plan for a new working partnership.

I missed work the next day, due to what someone (like Ellie Prosser) might consider a subconsciously self-fulfilling wish. An unfair assessment, to be sure. The accident was hardly something I would or could have orchestrated. I was running late that morning, rushing to make my usual train. I jerked open the outer door of my apartment as I was turning to leave, and walked face-on into the dull edge of the heavy door.

'Bloody hell!' I reeled back from the door. Suddenly my rush for work wasn't important. For a few minutes I couldn't even remember what I was doing. I had to lie down, still wearing my coat, until the numbness cleared from my head and the pain set in. I felt blood, then saw it on my fingers.

My head felt light and woozy when I got up. A look in

the bathroom mirror showed my forehead deeply abraded, and thick layers of skin scraped from the right cheek. It looked uglier than it probably was – with the paint chips and all. I put gauze over the wound, but I didn't have any medical tape to hold it down and, in any event, it was quickly soaked with blood. I shook my head – which didn't help the pain – in disbelief. It looked like I was going to be late.

Hours later I returned from the hospital, glaring at the undamaged, vicious apartment door as I entered. With stitches, clean dressings and an ice pack, the wounds would heal just fine. In the meantime, however, I'd have a couple of weeks of bandages and scabs and colourful bruises – including a blackened eye (as the doctor guaranteed), which I hadn't expected and which meant no contact lens and therefore severely limited vision until I could wear my glasses comfortably. I'd even had to be x-rayed to determine whether my cheekbone was fractured. Who'd have thought opening a door could do so much damage? What an idiot! Where was my mind? I knew people reacted to emotional trauma differently, but I surely wasn't using Dad's death as an excuse for self-mutilation. And I really wasn't trying to get out of that day's meeting.

I called Jack first to explain what had happened and let him know I wouldn't be in, then I asked Lorna to fax me the agenda and any notes for the afternoon meeting. She could also photocopy and fax the lay-outs I was supposed to review and the relevant body of photos under consideration. When we were finished setting up our game plan, she transferred me to Ellie Prosser.

'Where the hell are you, McDermott?' she demanded. 'You'd better not be trying to make a point about working from outside the office. Now is not the time. We've got to get this issue together today and I need you here.'

'Sorry, Ellie. There's no way I could make it there in time

for the meeting. I just got back from the hospital.'

'Hospital?' she grumbled. 'What have you been up to, McDermott?'

'Not to worry, the x-rays were good. Nothing worse than a hairline fracture. I'll be back in tomorrow. I'll tell you all about it then, stupid as it is.'

'But what about the meeting today? I can't put it off to accommodate you.'

'Relax, Prosser. You'll have my input. My secretary's faxing the material to me, and I'll be joining you by phone – after I've finished my own meeting with an ice pack.'

The ice pack, drugs and a twenty-minute nap recharged my energy in time for the teleconference, although really my presence was not vital. The meeting went off better than I'd expected. There was less to do than Ellie would have me believe. At that late stage in production, the remaining work was fine-tuning, and I'd already e-mailed my changes and faxed back my mark-ups for Jack to bring to the meeting. He held his own in my fellow editors' negotiations over individual space requirements. A few common interests were discussed. I gave my vote on which of the prospective covers I preferred. We all reported progress on upcoming issues. And then the meeting was over – longer than it needed to be, yet in no sense out of the ordinary.

'Great work, Tom,' said Jack as the group enjoyed minor social exchanges before returning to their departments. 'The text and the graphics seemed to transmit all right from here. Did you manage the material all right on your end?'

'No problem at all,' I said, grinning in spite of the pain. 'I could do it with one eye closed.'

25

THE WINDING-DOWN

Friday morning found me in Ellie Prosser's office, sipping on a cup of strong black coffee. My injuries were largely hidden by the sunglasses I continued to wear indoors – for appearance in part, and to compensate for increased photosensitivity from the black eye.

'Take those glasses off,' Ellie commanded. 'I need to see you when I'm talking to you.' So I removed the sunglasses. 'What happened, anyway? I didn't think you were the kind to get into fights.'

'Domestic violence,' I answered. 'I was attacked by my apartment door.'

'Umm,' she grunted. It wasn't a very exciting explanation. But, as improbable as my story might sound, she accepted the likelihood that it was true.

I looked her straight in the eye. 'Did you have something you wanted to follow up on from yesterday's meeting?'

'Not exactly,' she said. She was frowning at me. 'Oh, put

the glasses back on! It makes my eyes water looking at your face.'

'Thanks,' I said, smiling. 'I think you're lovely too.'

'Okay, okay,' she laughed. 'No, it's not about anything we covered at the meeting. That went well enough, I guess. Better than I expected.'

I kept silent, waiting for her to continue.

She sighed. 'It's time for the bottom line, Tom. What's this working-outside-the-office nonsense all about? Is this the first step towards leaving *Heights*?'

It hadn't occurred to me that she might think I was phasing myself out.

'No. Of course not, no.' Then I paused to reconsider my answer. 'I mean, not leaving this job. Although I've been thinking about giving up my apartment. I could use a shake-up in my domestic setting. The door accident may be a sign that it's time to move on, in that sense. An omen?'

Prosser leaned forward – a sure and rare sign of the intensity of her interest in the topic at hand. 'Cards on the table, Tom. Who made you an offer?'

I leaned forward in my chair, taking off the sunglasses again. 'You can look me in the eye, Ellie. The good one, with the contact lens.'

'Well?'

'No one has made me a job offer. Not recently, in any event.'

Her forehead began creasing, so I quickly clarified. 'Of course I'm approached from time to time, by our competitors. Headhunted. That's to be expected for anyone who's worth his salt . . . What I mean is that I don't have any offers under consideration. While I might continue to listen to any future offers politely, I don't expect to follow up on them. I'm not looking to leave *Heights*. And I'm not jockeying to rise within the company to some administrative level with no hands-on responsibilities, in case that possibility has also crossed your mind. I like working for the magazine. I love the work I do. I know it would take quite a bit of adjusting to not being in the office every day, to not having constant in-person contact with everyone here. But I honestly believe that I can bring more to my work – both the editing and writing – from the field than from a desk down the hall. In any event, it's something I feel I have to try.'

'You're being straight?'

'Absolutely.'

'And you think Jack's ready to take on more responsibilities?'

'I know he's ready. I have no reason to suspect that Jack's looking anywhere else either, but he's got to advance somewhere – with somebody else if not with us. Now, if we can advance him to co-editorship, under the terms we've sketched out, he'll have a rise in position, will still be able to supervise and contribute articles himself, and whatever travelling he may have to do will be primarily local. His daughter is young and he wants to be able to spend as much time with his family as possible. No other publisher's going to offer him such an ideal arrangement. Not any publisher of our status.'

She was drumming her pen on the desk again. 'And if your arrangement doesn't work out? Will you come back in-house?'

'It will work, Ellie. I won't give up *Heights*.'

She looked hard into my eyes – even the blackened one. When she was convinced that I believed everything I said was true, her expression calmed and she leaned back in her chair.

'All right, Tom,' she said. 'Let's go over your proposal. In detail.'

By the end of the following week, I'd sold Prosser on the

change of positions – Jack in-house and me in the field, as *Heights'* co-editors for arts and entertainment. The proposal was implemented almost immediately. No reason to delay.

In the meantime, for no explicable reason, my personal life remained an anonymous existence in a characterless apartment in a place called Hull. Should I stay in Hull? Should I look for another suburban community in New York? Or Connecticut or New Jersey or Pennsylvania? Should I live closer to the city? Closer to an airport? I hadn't started hunting for another apartment anywhere. I did nothing about getting rid of my motel-decor furniture. Between the possessions I'd accumulated in Hull and those I'd inherited in Magilligan, I'd developed quite a problem with property disposal.

I had to figure out what to do with myself in the here and now. Although I had put myself in a position where I'd no longer be tied to a nine-to-five Madison Avenue office grind or a five-days-a-week commute into the city, what I'd achieved in return was nebulous. Right as rain, perhaps, but nebulous. I was less rooted than I'd been since the early post-college years. Henceforth, if all went well, I would be essentially a freelance operant with a steady salary – an unusual situation contrived by my own efforts. I'd achieved the independence I wanted, but somehow the context was incomplete – as though I were free to sing my own song but didn't know the words.

I'd been in this funk for days since leaving the office. I was working steadily from home, in the gloomy apartment in Hull. So far the quality of my work, my level of creativity had not exactly soared. On late nights or early mornings when I couldn't sleep, I listened to old, sad songs or the kind of folksy blues I like to sing – or would like to sing, that is, if I had a piano at hand and weren't confined by flimsy apartment walls. (I did enjoy being called on to sing back in Ireland.) In the past few weeks I'd taken to regular long walks in the evening – something I'd never been prone to do before in all my years in Hull. The way my mind drifted while I wandered, sometimes I couldn't say whether I was actually walking along the deserted streets of Hull or the even quieter roads of Magilligan.

Somnus brevis III

REVISITING AN OLD ANCESTOR

*'Thomas Sean McDermott,' a voice called to me. It was the
red-haired young man I'd dreamed about before – my ancestor
from the fairy realm who could easily pass for my
present-day cousin Kieran Finney.*

'Seán Sylvanus Finney,' I responded in recognition. 'We
meet again. It's been a few years by your time, yes?'

'You were on the mark,' he said. 'I've done all right, after
all. Today there are four generations following me in my
own lifetime – my children, their children, and so on.'

'You don't look a day older than when I first saw you,' I
said, exaggerating only a little. If he was in his mid-twenties
before, in the earlier dream, he now looked no older than
twenty-seven or twenty-eight. Thirty at the outside.

'That's been well over a century ago,' he said. I must then
be visualising him sometime in the earlier or mid-eighteenth
century. 'Human years run too quickly, don't you think?'

'Are you still alive, then, in my time?'

'Not as such . . .' He thought a while. 'That's difficult to answer. This particular physical body no longer exists in your time.'

'But the spirit?'

'You do believe in reincarnation?'

'Yes,' I answered.

'Good,' he said. 'You, of all people, definitely should.'

'Are you Kieran then, as well – in my time?'

He didn't answer. The trend appeared to be that, if I figured out the truth, he wouldn't say. At least that's how I interrupted his lack of response.

Instead he motioned for me to follow. I did, through an underground maze of concrete walls, corridors, empty or filled with boxes or loose paraphernalia stacked against either wall. We ascended a metal, industrial stairwell into a storeroom crowded with dummies, mannequins, in varying states of nakedness or dress. At the other end we went up a wrought-iron spiral staircase to find ourselves standing in a gigantic research facility – resembling at once the old reading room in the British Museum and the New York Public Library, yet futuristic, with a curved glass roof overhead, controlled temperature and humidity, and rows of bookshelves, files, tables and computers. Seán waited for me to take it all in – a researcher's paradise. Then, all too soon, he led me across the chamber and up another set of stairs – these, mahogany and balustraded.

We emerged above ground – well above, in the panelled hallway of a multi-storeyed stone house sitting on top of a hill. The front door of the house stood open to the elements, open to a panoramic view of rolling, verdant hills and the steady undulations of the open sea beyond. The air was warm and sunny, and a breeze susurrated through wild flowers and whin bushes. I heard the baa-ing of sheep and the clomping of cows in the field. Somewhere a dog barked as it ran through the hillside.

'Where are we?' I asked.

'Another family residence. Come.'

Turning back to the hallway, I noticed a painting on the wall – eighteenth-century by style, painted in recent years.

'That's you,' I said, nodding towards the portrait of a couple. The woman portrayed with him was undoubtedly the lady who'd become his wife.

'Julia,' he identified her. 'You'll meet her another time.'

He didn't comment on the other paintings hanging in the hallway, but I scanned them quickly and noted the different styles. Some were local landscapes, many were portraits featuring other family members. A number were definitely Victorian and few distinctly late twentieth century.

I followed Seán into a good-sized end room brightened by large open-draped windows and scented by a low-burning turf fire in the hearth. He gestured and I sat on a cushioned sofa, glancing as I did so at a small open chest on a side table – a treasure trove of sea shells and smooth stones and palm-sized toys and keepsakes.

As he sat down, Seán spread a stack of albums on the table in front of us. He opened the volumes at random, to photos from all ages of the graphic and photographic arts. There were sketches and daguerreotypes, photogravures and other photographic images. There were stacks of the kinds of photos I grew up with – the old, square, serrated-edged black-and-white shots, and later white-bordered and borderless colour prints. Hundreds pasted into albums. Portraits of my family – my cousins, uncles, the grandparents in old age and youth. Ancestors I'd never seen but could recognise by physical traits or intuition. I could almost see myself in some of those faces.

Among the more recent material were pictures of my dad and his brothers, including the framed print in my bedroom. I saw another photo of the boys when they were grown, standing by their mother and father – probably taken just before Dad left Ireland.

Nor were the women neglected. The lovely Alice Flaherty was pictured with cousin Jamie. May McDermott (who would die in her youth) was represented, as were Great Aunt Maddy McDermott Connors and her family, Vinnie Finney and her late husband Marcus, and the Willoughbys.

Along with the young people in Dad's generation, there was an impossible shot of me with my cousins Walker and Kieran – impossible because we'd never been together at the same time and in the same place – looking for all the world like brothers assembled at some social gathering. And there were other photos that had never been taken in real life – including one of Marnie and me, seated on a rock in Greencastle, before a backdrop of Lough Foyle and the Magilligan Strand.

'How many of these pictures come from the future? From my future?' I asked. 'Or are they entirely fictional?'

Instead of answering the question, he told me: 'There are other galleries you might like to see.'

'Another time. I know,' I responded. But I wasn't in a hurry. Before I awoke to the less confusing and less interesting world of Hull-on-Hudson, I wanted to capture all the pleasures of this dream world, my ancestor's world. The setting, the room I was in, looked nothing like my study in Magilligan, but it felt the same. And I felt like a ghost haunting my family's homes.

26

THE DOPE FROM JACK

My black eye cleared up quickly although it was still sensitive, particularly to bright lights. The dark rainbow colours of bruised flesh faded. My face still bore stitch marks and patches of scabby dark red skin that made me look like I'd been in a fight.

I was recovering and, I thought, finally adapting to a new life style to accommodate my new work arrangement. The truth of the story was that I'd only been away from the *Heights* office for a week or so. Other than working from a makeshift home office, so far I hadn't made the slightest effort to establish myself as a creative, in-the-field editor. No *post-partum* depression for me after birthing my great work scheme; I was merely avoiding traumatic decisions. Yes, I was right that a greater potential lay in my operating outside the bounds of a four-walled office in Manhattan. To balance the equation, however, I had to make changes in my personal life; nothing was gained by my being based in Hull.

The difficulty with making changes in my personal life was that I'd actually have to address my personal life head-on – something I'd successfully avoided for a number of years. I dare say my house was not in order. But at least I'd clarified the nature of my problem.

For the past few days I'd been generally out of sync – nothing significant, just missed encounters. There was a trade show in Manhattan where I'd planned to catch up on news with a colleague from another magazine – more socialising than business. My train ran late, and my friend had to leave before I arrived. While I was at the conference, I missed a call from Sharon, who was returning from an undisclosed errand in White Plains and was close enough for us to have got together for a late lunch – except that by then I was already en route to Manhattan. Omens again? I wondered.

Since I was already feeling disjointed, I stopped by the Irish pub in Hull that I'd visited earlier. The bartender remembered me – as the fellow from Derry. I had a brief chat with an expatriate who'd be leaving in a couple of days for an extended Christmas holiday back in Dublin. And I noticed that the Irish regulars at the bar, who had previously favoured bottles of Budweiser, were tonight drinking pints of Guinness. I shook my head. What should I make of those changes. More portents?

One day Jack, now officially my co-editor, called about a freelance contribution he wanted to review with me – a newcomer's interview with a rising cabaret performer, an interview the author, a Margot Williams, had snagged through determination and with virtually no credentials. I talked Jack into making me a photocopy instead of faxing it. I'd meet him for a drink after work, somewhere near his home train station. Now that I was in a position where I didn't need to be in the presence of my office colleagues,

I wanted to see Jack face to face. I missed him. I was so deprived of company that I even missed Prosser.

That evening I drove over to Connecticut, to Greenwich, to meet Jack at a new, semi-trendy restaurant, where we could pig out on high-cholesterol hors d'oeuvres. We settled in at the bar rather than a table – just like we used to do for lunches in the city. Besides, it's chummier having a confab with a mate over a few pints at the bar.

I should describe Jack in greater detail. Better late in the game than not at all. Like Marnie, Jack's somewhat of a homebody. Like Sharon, he's devoted to his family. Like Paul the photographer, Jack is an artist in an inconspicuous way. One might legitimately guess that Jack's a member of Manhattan's corporate world. He looks corporate. More precisely, he looks like a department-store catalogue model of a young executive. That is to say, he fits the bill in the imagery department. Beyond appearance, however, he's remarkably well-studied in his craft and surprisingly artistic, having majored in journalism and minored in theatre. In college he was primarily interested in the business aspect of the theatre world, but his low-key approach and quick learning abilities made him a reliable stage actor. Nowadays his acting skills were limited to turning on the charm when conducting an interview and to enlivening the characters in the storybooks of Lucinda, his daughter. His friends also valued his natural exuberance. Not to mention a charming honesty.

'So,' he began, 'you're still here.'

'What do you mean?'

He looked at me. 'You haven't given up your apartment, have you?'

'Not exactly. Not yet . . . Was I supposed to?'

'That's the impression you gave.' He picked up his beer and clinked his glass against mine. 'Cheers.'

'Cheers.' I sighed. 'Now tell me about this Margot

Williams. Is her article any good?'

'Oh yes, very good. You'll see.' He handed me the copy he had rolled up in his jacket pocket. 'There's no question about using it. The only question is whether she's a one-time fluke, or should we cultivate her as a regular contributor?'

I raised an eyebrow. 'That good, is she?'

'You tell me,' he responded.

'I will,' I said, rolling the papers and stuffing them into my pocket. 'So how have you been, Jack?'

He told about little Lucinda's latest antics; he told me he and Amy were thinking about having another baby. He told me that I hadn't missed anything much in the office. I'd been in daily contact via phone and e-mail, and knew at least the highlights of everything that was going on at work.

'How about you, Tom?'

'How about what about me?'

'You're stalling. When are you making the move? A few people have already lost the office pool.'

I frowned. 'What's this office pool?'

'It's about when you're leaving Hull. Some of the people in Accounting expected you to be gone by now. They have you down as the impatient type. I guess that says something about your dealings with them.'

'I never said . . .' I began to protest. It was pointless. Time to yield to the general concensus. 'What date do you have?' I asked.

He shook his head. 'I was declared ineligible. As were Ellie and Lorna . . . But I would have given you about two weeks. Or, more fittingly in your case, a fortnight.'

'Just about now,' I remarked. 'And where would you all have me moving to? Or is that the subject of another office pool?'

'You're kidding,' he answered. His quizzical look was sincere.

'No,' I said. 'I'm not.' At times I'm very obtuse, especially when communicating with myself.

He looked at me with a knowing smile but didn't say anything. After another swallow of his beer he excused himself to visit the men's room. As he walked away, I could hear him singing 'Danny Boy' under his breath.

27

MY FATHER'S VOICE

Another weekend arrived. Somehow the weekends still felt different than the five intervening workdays, even though I wasn't in the office. I'd been all day Saturday, buying groceries, looking over books I wasn't really interested in, and driving along back roads that only led to other sleepy, nameless towns. I saw cut Christmas trees being sold at lots that lay vacant the rest of the year. Large evergreens stood – tall, colourfully lit – before town halls and fire stations. Lights and street-lamp ornaments lined the high streets of every small community. The Hudson River was ever-so-noticeably choppy – thicker in consistency, I imagined, with December's lower temperatures. Visibility decreased as a wet, sleet-bearing mist descended with the night.

My clothes were damp from being outdoors in the wet, heavy sleet that turned to slush when it hit the ground. Back inside, I draped my coat over a chair next to a rattling radiator – my substitute for a hearth fire. The room smelled of the wet fabric. I pulled on a warm, dry sweater and poured a welcome glass of whisky. In the mail was a small package from Ireland. A paperback *The Midnight Dog* by Kieran Finney. The cover featured an isolated cottage lost in a swirling night-time blizzard. I chuckled. I had a feeling I'd enjoy reading this and thought I'd save it for bedtime.

I found myself wondering whether it had snowed yet in Magilligan. It was important to know. I couldn't bear the thought of missing the first snow of the season there. I wished I could watch it from the windows in the study. With a turf fire burning. Perhaps a sip of smoky whisky.

I thought about how my preconceptions, my misconceptions about Ireland (at least the small area I was getting to know) had already changed. My mind was aclutter with issues of terrorism, cease-fires, Catholic and Protestant concerns, British and Irish governments, the effects of devolution in Scotland and Wales on Northern Ireland, and all the questions of Northern Ireland's identity. At the end of the day, it all came down to peace. The people wanted peace.

As for my own family, they were as much a hodgepodge as I could ever imagine – crossing religious lines, spanning political borders, conservative and liberal, outspoken and stoic. Not to mention the legends of reputed supernatural ancestry that was all part of the mix. Culturally, we had musicians – singers and players – but few dancers. Some drinkers, some teetotallers. Some family members were gregarious, some were quiet. They were diverse. Their history, my history, mixed pride and shame, fantasy and reality. In short, they were a lovely people in a lovely land. I was glad, after all, to be part of them to any extent. I liked being with them and . . .

My mental ramblings were disturbed by the radiator rattling under the window. The interruption reminded me that I'd meant to do something more interesting than watching the steam rise. I didn't try the television programmes. Surely I could find something better by rummaging through my video cabinet. In the back row there were older, home-produced tapes from my youth and college days. I grabbed one labelled 'Oakdale – Summer – Christmas Vacation' and put it in the player.

The tape began with the end of my first year at Oakdale College. We were packing to leave and generally partying around exam schedules. All those faces, my dorm mates. Most of them I never saw again after college.

Next was Dad's place, in Scranton. It was many years after the divorce. I stayed with Dad that summer, the last summer before I was living on my own, and worked at Diedrich's, which was still Dad's store then. Dad filmed us in the park. Me and Woody, an old dog by that time. Playing catch with a well-slobbered old tennis ball.

Back in Dad's apartment, I had control of the camera. Woody was asleep on his own oval rag rug. Dad was at the piano, singing in his steady, unassuming tenor voice. 'You'll Never Know' was the song. I didn't remember having this recording. I gave it my rapt attention. I watched to the end.

There was something sad in the song, just as there was always a trace of something sad in Dad. I knew he was reluctant to leave his family, his home in Magilligan; he regretted leaving before he'd even gone. But he did go, to earn a living and make a new life in America. He did his best. He fell in love and married. He worked hard until he took over Diedrich's and then just as hard to keep it profitable. He provided well for his family until the divorce, for Mom until she remarried, and for me. He provided for me my entire life. As much as he must have wanted to when he was young, he didn't go back home until I was well established in a career. And he was dying.

I wished that I could know the home he had loved and

missed all those years, the home he'd left for me across the ocean. He might have told me: 'You'll never know if you don't know now.' Or perhaps he did tell me that on the tape.

The song ended. I stopped the tape. 'You'll Never Know' was Dad's song. I wasn't going to make mine 'I Ain't Got No Home'. Or the 'How Long Blues?'

There was no point in wasting time wishing I had what was waiting for me across the Atlantic. What difference did it make where I telecommuted from? I had family well beyond the family I visited in Scranton on holidays. I had a home. I had the chance to combine the best of two worlds. It could be a rich life – if I took the chance and made the effort, and if the fates were truly with me.

If I started packing right away, I could be home in Magilligan before the first snowfall.